"Singer's stories have plots that unravel not [...]
they are mostly originals and have few reco [...]
own—but because they contain the whole human world of affliction, [...],
quagmire, pain, calamity, catastrophe, woe: things happen; life is an ambush,
a snare; one's fate can never be predicted. His driven, mercurial processions of
predicaments and transmogrifications are limitless, a cornucopia of invention."

CYNTHIA OZICK

"[Singer] is a spellbinder as clever as Scheherazade; he arrests the reader at
once, transports him to a far place and a far, improbable time and does not let
him go until the end."

JEAN STAFFORD, *THE NEW REPUBLIC*

"A peerless storyteller, Singer restores the sheer enchantment with story, with
outcome, with what-happens-next that has been denied most readers since
their adolescence."

DAVID BOROFF, *SATURDAY REVIEW*

"Singer is a genius. He has total command of his imagined world."

IRVING HOWE, *THE NEW REPUBLIC*

"Extraordinarily beautiful. . . . It's the integrity of the human imagination that
Singer conveys so beautifully."

ALFRED KAZIN, *THE NEW LEADER*

BOOKS BY ISAAC BASHEVIS SINGER

NOVELS

The Family Moskat (1950) • *Satan in Goray* (1955) • *The Magician of Lublin* (1960) • *The Slave* (1962) • *The Manor* (1967) • *The Estate* (1969) • *Enemies, a Love Story* (1972) • *Shosha* (1978) • *The Penitent* (1983) • *The King of the Fields* (1988) • *Scum* (1991) • *The Certificate* (1992) • *Meshugah* (1994) • *Shadows on the Hudson* (1997)

STORY COLLECTIONS

Gimpel the Fool and Other Stories (1957) • *The Spinoza of Market Street* (1961) • *Short Friday and Other Stories* (1963) • *The Séance and Other Stories* (1968) • *A Friend of Kafka and Other Stories* (1970) • *The Fools of Chelm and Their History* (1973) • *A Crown of Feathers and Other Stories* (1974) • *Passions and Other Stories* (1975) • *Old Love: Stories* (1979) • *The Collected Stories* (1982) • *The Image and Other Stories* (1985) • *The Death of Methuselah and Other Stories* (1988)

BOOKS FOR CHILDREN

Zlateh the Goat and Other Stories (1966) • *Mazel and Shlimazel* (1967) • *The Fearsome Inn* (1967) • *When Shlemiel Went to Warsaw and Other Stories* (1968) • *The Golem* (1969) • *Elijah the Slave: A Hebrew Legend Retold* (1970) • *Joseph and Koza: or the Sacrifice to the Vistula* (1970) • *Alone in the Wild Forest* (1971) • *The Topsy-Turvy Emperor of China* (1971) • *The Wicked City* (1972) • *The Fools of Chelm and Their History* (1973) • *Why Noah Chose the Dove* (1974) • *A Tale of Three Wishes* (1975) • *Naftali and the Storyteller and His Horse, Sus* (1976) • *Reaches of Heaven: A Story of the Baal Shem Tov* (1980) • *The Power of Light: Eight Stories for Hanukkah* (1980) • *Stories for Children* (1984) • *Shrew Todie and Lyzer the Miser and Other Children's Stories* (1994) • *The Parakeet Named Dreidel* (2015)

NONFICTION

In My Father's Court (1967) • *A Day of Pleasure, Stories of a Boy Growing Up in Warsaw* (1969) • *Love and Exile* (1984) • *More Stories from My Father's Court* (1999) • *Old Truths and New Clichés: Essays* (2022)

Restless Books received support to publish this work from David Bruce Smith, Grateful American Foundation, and Terry Philip Segal, in honor of Joe Lieberman, who made modern Jewish orthodoxy mainstream in American life.

Simple Gimpl

ISAAC BASHEVIS SINGER

· The Definitive Bilingual Edition ·

TRANSLATIONS BY

Isaac Bashevis Singer, Saul Bellow, and David Stromberg

Illustrations by Liana Finck

Afterword by David Stromberg

RESTLESS BOOKS

BROOKLYN, NEW YORK

"Simple Gimpl" first published in Yiddish as גימפל תם in *Idisher kempfer*, 1945

First Restless Books hardcover edition February 2023

Hardcover ISBN: 9781632060389
Library of Congress Control Number: 2022948923

Cover design by Aubrey Nolan
Cover illustration by Liana Finck
Text design and layout by Tetragon, London

Printed in Italy

1 3 5 7 9 10 8 6 4 2

Restless Books, Inc.
232 3rd Street, Suite A101
Brooklyn, NY 11215

www.restlessbooks.org
publisher@restlessbooks.org

CONTENTS

EDITOR'S NOTE

"Gimpl tam," as it is known in its Yiddish original, is one of the most iconic short stories of the twentieth century. It might be said to have defined the way Americans—in particular, American Jews—ultimately looked at the world destroyed by the Holocaust. First published in Yiddish at the end of the Second World War, it auspiciously arrived in English in 1953, in Saul Bellow's translation published in *Partisan Review*.

The birth of that translation is surrounded in controversy. Literary critics Irving Howe and Eliezer Greenberg were under contract to edit the anthology *A Treasury of Yiddish Stories* (1954). Greenberg gave "Gimpl tam" to Howe. Howe, in turn, asked Saul Bellow, who was born in Canada and had been raised in a Yiddish household, to bring it into English. By most accounts, Bellow translated the story in a single sitting, said to have lasted around three hours. He titled it "Gimpel the Fool." Bellow might not have even written it down himself, since, according to one account, he dictated it to Greenberg. There are also suggestions that Bellow's Yiddish wasn't fully fluent, which explains, in part, the liberties he took, starting with the title: the Yiddish word "*tam*," which comes from Hebrew, doesn't mean fool; yet the rhyming of "Gimpel the Simple" was, well, foolish. At any rate, translation *is* about freedom. Bellow's style is everywhere in "Gimpl tam." That might help explain the story's immediate and far-reaching acclaim. He was the up-and-coming author of *Dangling Man* and *The Victim*, and about to publish *The Adventures of Augie March*, which would go on to receive the National Book Award.

Even though the story joined these two geniuses at the hip, the truth is that throughout their careers Singer and Bellow developed a courteous if tortured relationship, keeping each other at arm's length—especially Singer, who, as he made clear in letters and interviews, was jealous of Bellow. Born in 1903, Singer was more than a decade older, a Polish-born Jewish immigrant to New York, isolated in the parochial enclave of Yiddish-speaking refugees from Europe, whereas Bellow, who was born in 1915, was widely recognized as a luminous Jewish intellectual, at home in the English language, and part of a cadre that was redefining American letters. Although a novel by Singer, *The Family Moskat*, had been translated into English previously, it had gone nowhere. The fact that Singer ultimately found his footing in America thanks to Bellow's translation of "Gimpl tam" made him uncomfortable for years. Add to it that he received the Nobel Prize in 1978, two years after Bellow, and you have the reasons for his simmering discomfort.

The register of "Gimpl tam" is somewhere between a fable and a folk tale. Singer portrays the shtetl as a conniving place. Having a simpleton as the first-person narrator is a winning strategy: tempted by evil and incapable of decoding his surroundings, he chooses the higher ground. In the mid-fifties, readers responded to Gimpl with a mix of awe—in his nearsightedness, he was a sage—as well as nostalgia for what Singer's older brother Israel Joshua called "a world that is no more." Since then, all sorts of interpretations have accrued: about the nature of truth, about the endurance of Jewish diaspora life, and about what justifies revenge.

In Singer's old age he himself took a stab at rendering the story into English, producing a draft for dramatization. The present volume features that rendition, called "Simple Gimpl," completed by writer, translator, and scholar David Stromberg, along with an afterword by Stromberg explaining his discovery of the journal that featured it, his view on the story's history, and his take on the piece's crucial aspects. The "new" version is followed by Bellow's translation and then by Singer's Yiddish original. They are accompanied by Liana Finck's gorgeous illustrations, in themselves another interpretation of "Gimpl tam." This structure not only puts Singer and Bellow in dialogue—even if reluctantly—but looks at how the story has been appreciated across generations. It also celebrates translation as an integral component of world literature, for without it, entire civilizations would disappear irrevocably. And then there's the question of self-translation. When authors opt to render their own work in another language, what is gained or lost?

A note on style in Singer's story: his Yiddish, both idiosyncratic and colloquial, has been standardized according to YIVO guidelines. Still, a couple of elements have required judgment calls. One is about word variants. Two words are used frequently but inconsistently: "*ton*" and "*zenen*"—roughly, "do" and "were." Both have a standardized form and a recognized and acceptable Polish regional variant. In both cases, Singer used both variants, seemingly at random. Stylistically, this was problematic. An English analogy would be: "favor" vs. "favour," or "honor" vs. "honour." Our call was to use the regional variant throughout. The other element relates to Singer's approach to marking quotations. Yiddish literary style uses em-dashes to set quotations apart. Singer does this sometimes, but at other times he just uses a colon before a quote, and sometimes just a comma. This is unconventional, but given the colloquial tone, some of the quotations appear to "fit" more within the flow of the text, making the styling intentional. This does not violate the standard and so it was left as it appeared in the original publication.

—*Ilan Stavans*

Simple Gimpl

Translated from the Yiddish
by Isaac Bashevis Singer
and David Stromberg

ONE

I'm Simple Gimpl. I don't consider myself a fool. Quite the opposite. But that's the nickname I was given.

This is what they've called me since Hebrew school. Like Jethro, I had seven nicknames: jerk, jackass, moron, idiot, nincompoop, sucker, simpleton. The last name stuck. You want to know why? Because I was easily deceived. Someone said, "You know, Gimpl, the rabbi's wife is giving birth," and I didn't go to Hebrew school. Well, it turned out to be a lie. How was I supposed to know? Because she didn't have a big belly? Well, I didn't go looking at her belly. Is that foolish?

3

But the wise guys laughed and poked fun. They danced around, calling out, "The Lord's a King—and you're a jackass." And instead of handing out raisins, like you do after a woman gives birth, they stuffed my hands with goat turds. Anyone can see I'm not weak. If I landed a punch, you'd see to Kraków. But it wasn't in my nature to be a tough guy. So I forgot about it. Let it pass. And they picked on me.

Once, on the way home from school, I heard a dog barking. I'm not afraid of dogs, but there's no point goading them on. It could be a wild dog, and if it bites you, you're done for. So I got out of there. I looked around. The whole marketplace was laughing. Well, it wasn't really a dog. It was Wolf Leyb the Thief, may he rest in pieces. How was I supposed to know? He sounded every bit like a howling bitch.

When the wise guys realized that I was gullible, they all began to try their luck. "Gimpl, the Kaiser's coming to Frampol." "Gimpl, the moon fell down in Turbin." "Gimpl, Hodele Lambskin found a treasure behind the bathhouse." And, like a jerk, I believed them. First of all, anything is possible, as it says in the *Ethics* . . . I don't remember where. Second, when the whole town's picking on you, you have to believe. If I ever tried saying, "Hey, you're making it up," things got even worse. They'd get all fired up. "What's with you? You don't believe us? You think Frampol's full of liars?" What was I supposed to do? I believed—and let the clowns have a good time.

I was an orphan. My grandfather, who raised me, was already smelling the soil. I was apprenticed to a baker. And don't ask what they did to me there. Every woman, old and young, who came to bake cookies or to dry noodles, had to trick me at least once. "Gimpl, there's a fair going on in heaven." "Gimpl, the rabbi calved in the seventh month." "A cow flew over the roof and laid brass eggs."

A yeshiva student once came to buy plum cake and said, "You, Gimpl, are shoveling your oven paddle, and outside the Messiah has come. Corpses are being resurrected."

"How's that?" I said. "No one blew the ram's horn."

"Are you deaf?" he said.

And everyone called out, "We heard it, we heard, heard it."

While he was saying this, Reitze, the candlemaker, came in and with her hoarse voice called out, "Your parents have risen from their graves. They're looking for you."

I should really say that I knew very well it was completely impossible. Still, this is what they said.

I put on my coat and went outside. Maybe it was true. What did I have to lose?

You should have heard their howls and cries. I vowed never to believe anything again. But that was no good either. They mixed me up so I didn't know whether I was coming or going.

I left and went to the rabbi for advice.

He said, "It's written: better to be a jackass all your life than to be wicked for a single hour. You're no fool," he said. "They're the fools. Because if you shame another, you give up the world to come."

And yet the rabbi's own daughter tricked me. As I left his court, she said, "Have you kissed the wall yet?"

"No. What for?"

"There's such a law that if you come to the rabbi, you kiss the wall."

So, just to do it, I gave the doorpost a little peck. Did it cost me anything? And she let out a screeching laugh. The rabbi's daughter had pulled a fast one on Gimpl.

I was ready to move to another city, but people started talking to me about making a match. *Talking* about a match—they wouldn't let me go. I got water in my ears. She was a grown woman, but they insisted she was a young girl. She had a lame leg and walked with a limp—they convinced me she was being cute. She had a bastard, but they said it was her younger brother. I cried out, "You're wasting your time. I'm not going to marry this whore." But they insisted. "For such pretty talk, we'll take you to the rabbi and he'll fine you for sullying the reputation of a Jewish daughter." I saw that I couldn't escape their grasp. I thought, *Who cares! I'm the man, not she. And if she wants to, I'm willing.* Besides, you can't die a bachelor.

I went over to her limestone hut in the unpaved part of town, and everyone followed me like bear keepers. But when we reached the well they stopped. They were afraid to start anything with Elka. She had a mouth that moved a mile a minute. I went inside. The house was nothing but a hovel with no floors. From wall to wall, there were clotheslines hanging with laundry. She stood barefoot by the basin and did the washing. She was wearing a velvet dressing gown. She also wore two braids the way, forgive the comparison, a peasant girl does, twisted together on both sides. I could hardly breathe.

She seemed to know who I was, because she took one look at me and said, "What's this? The sucker's here. Take a stool and sit yourself down."

I told her everything, denied nothing.

"Tell me the truth," I said, "are you really a virgin, and is that little rascal Yehiel really your younger brother? Don't make fun of me," I said, "I'm an orphan."

"I'm an orphan too," she answered, "and anyone who makes fun of you should have fungus grow on his nose. But this town shouldn't think that they can make a fool of me. I want," she said, "a dowry of fifty guilders and wedding gifts too. If not, they can kiss my you-know-what." She used a bad word.

"The dowry's given by the bride," I said, "not the groom."

"Don't haggle with me," she said. "If it's yes, then yes. If no, then no—and go back to where you came from."

I was already thinking that you couldn't bake bread with this dough, but our town isn't poor. They gave her everything she asked for and planned the wedding. There was a cholera outbreak just then, and the wedding canopy was raised inside the cemetery, next to the shack where they wash the dead. The fellows got drunk. While the marriage contract was being made up, I heard the assistant rabbi ask, "Is the bride widowed or divorced?" "Both," answered the beadle's wife. I saw stars. But what was I supposed to do? Run out from under the wedding canopy?

People played music and started dancing. An old lady danced near me with a wedding loaf. The jester recited "God, full of mercy." Schoolkids threw thorns as if it were Tisha B'Av. There ended up being plenty of wedding presents: a noodle board, a trough, a grater, brooms, ladles, lots of things for the house. I looked and saw two young fellows bringing in a cradle. "Why a cradle?" I asked. They told me, "Don't wrack your brain. Everything's fine. It'll come in handy." I could see I was being sold a bill of goods. But then again, what did I have to lose? I thought, *I'll wait and see what happens. The whole town can't be crazy.*

TWO

That night I came to lie down next to my wife but she didn't let me in.

"What?" I said. "Isn't this why we got married?"

"I'm having my period," she said.

"What are you talking about?" I argued. "Only yesterday they led you to the ritual bath with musicians playing."

"Today isn't yesterday and yesterday isn't today. If you don't like it, you can clear out."

In short, I waited. No less than four months later, my wife was in labor. Everyone in Frampol laughed into their sleeves. But what was I supposed

11

to do? Her contractions were painful. She scratched at the walls. "Gimpl," she screamed, "I'm as good as gone. Forgive me!" Old women filled the house. They boiled water like they do for washing the dead. Her screams reached up to the heavens. So I went to the prayer house to recite psalms. The fellows needed nothing more. I stood in the corner pleading with God, and they nodded their heads. "Pray," they egged me on, "words never got anyone pregnant." One of the no-goods stuck a piece of straw in my mouth. "A jackass should eat straw." As I live, he too had a point.

With some luck she delivered the baby and had a boy. During Friday-evening prayers, the assistant rabbi stepped onto the synagogue platform, smacked the table, and called out, "The wealthy Reb Gimpl invites everyone to celebrate the birth of a boy." The whole prayer house laughed. It was a slap in the face. But what was I supposed to do? I was still the boy's father. Half the town came running. You couldn't stick in a single pin. Women brought peppered peas and a small barrel of beer was brought from the tavern. I ate and drank just like everyone else and they all wished me *mazel tov*. Afterward, they did the circumcision and I named the little one after my father, may he rest in peace.

When they all went home and I was left alone with the new mother, she stuck her head out from behind the curtain and called me to her bed.

"Gimpl," she said, "why so quiet? Did you lose a shipful of sour milk?"

"What's there to say?" I answered. "You really pulled a fast one. If my mother had lived to see it, she would have died all over again."

"Are you out of your mind or something?"

"How," I said, "could you make such a fool out of a man?"

"What's with you?" she asked. "What's gotten into your head?"

I could see that I had to talk straight. I said, "Is this how you treat an orphan? You've given birth to a bastard."

"Forget about such foolishness," she said. "It's your child."

"How could it be my child?" I argued. "You had it seventeen weeks after our wedding."

She told me stories about babies being born in the seventh month.

I said, "Seven is not five."

She started arguing that she had a grandmother who'd carried only five months, and that the two of them were as alike as two drops of water. She swore to it with such conviction that you'd have believed her like a hawker at a fair. Truth be told, I didn't believe her. But when I talked to the Hebrew teacher the next day, he said that such a thing was mentioned in the Gemara. Adam and Eve went to bed two and got out of bed four. "Well," he said, "every woman is a granddaughter of Mother Eve, so why isn't Elka as good as Eve?" One way or another, they pulled the wool over my eyes. On the other hand, who knows? After all, they say that little baby Jesus had no father at all.

Soon, I began to forget my misfortune. I loved the child immensely, and he loved me too. As soon as he saw me, he started waving his hands for me to take him. When he was upset, nobody could get him to sleep except for me. I bought him a teething ring made of bone and a little gold-lined cap. Every other day, people gave him the evil eye, and I was quick to ward it off. Meanwhile, I worked like a horse. You need more with a child in the house. And, to tell the truth, I didn't dislike Elka either. She cursed me and called me names, and I groveled to her.

She had such power! When she gave me one of her looks, I was paralyzed. And her expressions! She could let loose with fire and brimstone and it was somehow extremely charming. Worth kissing every word. She wormed her way into your heart, and you lay on the oven, all carved up like a roast, and wanting more. In the evening, besides bread, I also brought home hallah that I baked especially for her, and a few rolls. For her sake I became a thief and pinched whatever I could: a piece of cake here, a macaroon there, a raisin here and an almond there. I hope it's not held against me, but I opened someone's *cholent* pot, left to warm in my oven, and took out a strand of meat, a bit of *kugel*, a chicken head or leg, a piece of stuffed *derma*, whatever I could. She ate and grew pretty and plump. During the week, I didn't sleep at home. I'd come to her on Friday nights, but she always had an excuse. Once she had heartburn, and once her side hurt. Once she had the hiccups and once a headache. Not to mention the female matters! Don't ask how I suffered. On top of that, her brother, the bastard, kept growing. He'd hit me and when I wanted to give it back to him, she'd unleash her vengeful tongue so that my eyes saw green. Ten times a day she'd threaten me with divorce. I would have taken off to the hills, but my nature is to let things pass. What can you do? If God gave you shoulders, you have to carry the burden.

One night we had some trouble at the bakery: the oven burst and there was nearly a fire. Since I had nothing to do, I went home. *I wouldn't mind*, I thought, *having the pleasure of sleeping in my own bed on a regular weekday*. I didn't want to wake the little one, so I came in quietly on my tiptoes. I walked into the house and somehow I heard a double snoring. One thinner snore, and another as if from a slaughtered ox. I didn't like this story at all! I went over to the bed and my stomach turned: a man was lying next to Elka. Someone else in my position might have made a fuss—and half the town would have been there. But I thought, *Why wake the child? It's not the poor little bird's fault.* Anyway, I went back to the bakery and lay down on a sack of flour. I couldn't close my eyes until daybreak. I felt feverish. *Enough*, I thought, *of being a jackass. Gimpl will not let himself be sold a bill of goods anymore. There's a limit even to how much Gimpl can be duped.*

In the morning I went to the rabbi and raised the question with him. It made a lot of noise in town. They sent the rabbi's helper straight for her. My wife came with child in arms. And what do you think she did? Denied the whole thing. "He's lost his mind," she said. "I don't know anything about anything." They shouted at her, warned her, smacked the table, but she stuck to her own: This was a false accusation. The butchers and horse dealers stood by her. A young slaughterer came over to me and said, "Your days are numbered." Meanwhile the child got upset and soiled itself. There was a Holy Ark in the rabbi's courtroom so they sent her away.

I said to the rabbi, "What should I do?"

"You have to divorce her immediately."

"And if she refuses the divorce?"

"Give it to her anyway."

"Fine, Rabbi, I'll think it over."

"There's nothing to think about," he said. "You're not allowed to be under the same roof with her."

"And if I want to see the child?" I asked.

"You don't need to see the child," said the rabbi. "Let her go, that whore, together with her bastards!"

He pronounced a verdict that I was not even to cross her threshold. Never. Not as long as I lived.

It didn't bother me much during the day. *Well, anyway*, I thought, *the blister had to burst*. But at night, sleeping on the sacks, I felt terrible. I yearned for her, and for the child. I wanted to be angry with her, but that's my undoing: I can't be angry. *First of all*, I thought, *so what if a person does something foolish. That young no-good probably winked at her, gave her presents, and females are long on hair and short on wits, so she was persuaded. Secondly, if she denies it so strongly, maybe it was an illusion? It sometimes happens that you see a figure, like a little person, but when you get up close, it turns out to be nothing. In that case, she's the victim of an injustice.* As I thought this way, I started to cry. I wept so much that the flour got wet. Early in the morning I went to the rabbi's and said that I'd made a mistake. The rabbi set it all down with his quill and said he'd write about it to other rabbis for their opinion. Until then, I was not to go near my wife. But I could send her baked goods by messenger, and money for her to live on.

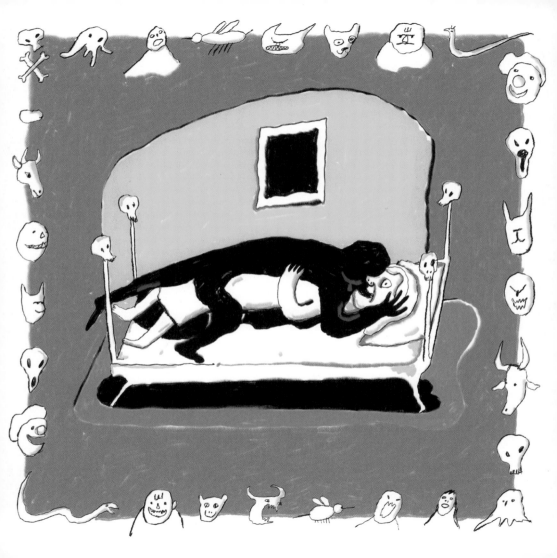

THREE

It took three-quarters of a year for the rabbis to come to an agreement. Letters went back and forth. I didn't know that there was so much Torah scholarship about such a matter. In the meantime, my Elka carried to term and had another child, a girl. On the Sabbath, I went to synagogue and recited a blessing for the mother. I was called up to recite the blessing for the reading of the Torah, and I named the child after my mother-in-law, may she rest in peace. The slackers who hung around the bakery had plenty to talk about. Everyone in Frampol reveled in my shame. But I made up my mind from that day on to believe everything. What do you gain by not believing? Today you don't believe your wife, tomorrow you won't believe in God.

Every day I sent her—with an assistant who lived nearby—some corn-bread, wheat bread, at times I added a currant cake, a roll, some egg bagels, and, when I had the chance, a slice of honey cake or other cakes that fell into my hands. The assistant was a good-hearted young man. More than once he added baked goods from his own share. Before this, he had started up with me, flicked my nose, poked me in the ribs. But once he started going to my house, he became as warm as a chest rub. "Hey you, Gimpl," he said to me, "you've got a good wife and two fine kids. You don't deserve them." "What about what people are saying?" "People have long tongues, so they wag them," he answered. "Pay no attention."

One day the rabbi sent for me and said, "Are you sure, Gimpl, that you were mistaken?"

"I'm sure, Rabbi."

"But," he said, "you saw it yourself."

"It must have been a shadow," I said.

"A shadow?" he asked. "Of what?"

And I said, "A roof beam."

"In that case," he said, "you may go back home. You should be grateful to the Yanover Rabbi. He found an obscure passage in Maimonides."

I grabbed the rabbi's hand and kissed it. At first I wanted to run straight home. It was no little thing not to see your wife and children for so long. Then I thought, *I'd better go back to work and go home at night*. I didn't say a word to anyone. But in my heart it was like a holiday. The girls and women teased and mocked me like they did every day, but I thought to myself, *Talk away. The truth will rise like oil on water. If Maimonides says "kosher"—it's kosher*.

That night, after covering the dough for it to rise, I took my share of bread, grabbed a sackful of sifted flour, and set out for home. There was a full moon in the sky and the stars twinkled as though their lives depended on it. I took long strides and up ahead a long shadow scurried along. It was winter and fresh snow had just fallen. I felt like singing, but it was late, and I didn't want to wake the respectable folk. I felt like whistling but remembered that you're not supposed to whistle at night because it summons the spirits. I was silent and marched as fast as I could. Dogs from the peasant yards heard my steps and started barking, but I thought, *Let them bark. You're dogs and I'm a person. The husband of a respectable wife, the father of bright children*.

I arrived at my little home and my heart was beating so loud you could hear it. I wasn't afraid, but my heart was pounding: *boom, boom*. Well, the die was cast. I took the chain silently off the door and stepped inside. Elka was already sleeping. I stood where I was and looked into the cradle. The shutter was closed but the moon shone in through the cracks. I saw the little girl's face and liked it from the first moment—just like that, all at once. I wanted to kiss every bone in her little body. Then I went to the bed. And what do you think I saw? Elka lying there, and next to her—the assistant. All at once the moon went out. My eyes went dark. My hands and feet trembled. My teeth started chattering. The bread fell out of my hands. My wife woke up and asked, "Who's there? Who is it?"

"It's me," I muttered.

"Gimpl?" she asked. "What are you doing here? Are you allowed?"

"The rabbi said I could," I answered, feeling feverish.

"Listen to me, Gimpl," she said. "Go outside to the shed and check on the goat. I think she's sick."

I forgot to mention that we had a goat. When I heard the nanny wasn't well, I went out to the yard. She was a good creature. I liked her, forgive the comparison, as though she were a person.

I went over to the shed with uneven steps and opened up the door.

The goat stood on four solid legs. I felt her all around, pulled her by the horns, put my hands on her udder. I didn't see anything wrong. Probably ate too much bark. "Good night to you, little goat," I said. "Stay healthy and strong." And the dumb animal answered with a "baa," as if to tell me, "Thank you very much."

I returned and saw that the assistant had run off.

"Where," I asked, "is the fellow?"

"What fellow?" asked my wife in response.

"The assistant," I said. "You were sleeping with him!"

"May the nightmares I had tonight and every other night," my wife called out, "come to haunt you. You must be possessed," she said, "by some evil spirit who has blinded you!" She yelled, "You jerk! You jackass! You mancalf! You moron! Get out of here, I'm warning you, or I'll let loose screaming until everyone in Frampol is here!"

Before I knew it, her brother jumped out from behind the oven and hit me with his fist right on the back of the head. I thought he'd break my neck. I understood that there was something wrong with me and I pleaded with her, "Don't turn me into a laughing stock. All I need," I said, "is for people to say that I have doings with evil spirits. No one would come near anything I baked." In short, I managed to calm her down.

"Well, it's over," she said, "so lie down and get crippled."

In the morning I called the assistant aside quietly. "Listen to me, brother," I said, "what were you doing in my wife's bed?" He looked at me as if I'd fallen off a roof. "As I live and breathe," he said, "you'd better go to a healer or an old peasant woman. I'm afraid," he said, "you've got a screw loose. But I'll let it pass. I won't say a thing. Mum's the word." And that's how we left things.

To make a long story short, I lived with my wife for over twenty years. She bore me six children, four girls and two boys. A lot happened during those years. But I saw nothing, heard nothing. I believed. That's all. The rabbi said the other day that when you believe, things are good. It's written that a righteous man lives by his faith.

All at once, my wife got sick. It started with something small, a lump on her breast. But it seemed she didn't have much time left. I spent a fortune on her. I forgot to say that by then I already had a bakery of my own and that, in Frampol, I was considered something of a wealthy man. The healer came every day. Wherever a sorceress was found, they brought her to us. They tried lancing, leeching, cupping. They even brought a doctor from Lublin. But it was too late.

Before her death, she called me to her bed and said, "Gimpl, forgive me."

"What's there to forgive?" I said. "You were a loyal wife."

"Oh no, my poor Gimpl," she said. "I deceived you shamelessly all those years. I want to go to God clean. You should know that the children are not yours."

If I'd been hit over the head with a roof beam, I would have been less confused.

"So whose are they?"

"I don't know," she said. "There were many. But yours they are not."

And as she said this, she turned her head, rolled her eyes, and Elka was no more. On her white lips there was still a smile. It seemed to me that with her death she was saying, "I deceived Gimpl. This was the meaning of my short life."

FOUR

Once, at night, after the seven days of mourning, while I lay on the sacks dozing, something seemed to come to me, the Evil Spirit itself, and said, "Gimpl, why are you sleeping?"

"What should I be doing," I said, "eating dumplings?"

"The whole world is deceiving you," it said. "Deceive the world!"

"How can I deceive the whole world?"

"Collect a pail of urine every day," it answered, "and every night, pour it into the dough. Let them," it said, "devour filth, those Frampol wise guys."

"What about the next world?" I said.

It said, "There is no next world. They've sold you a pig in a poke."

"Well," I said, "and is there a God?"

"There's no God either."

"So what," I said, "is there?"

"A deep mire."

It stood before my eyes, this orator, with a goat's beard and horns, long teeth and a tail. Hearing this kind of talk, I tried to grab it by the tail, but I fell off the flour sacks, and almost broke a rib. I happened to need to urinate and noticed a big piece of dough that seemed to be begging: *Do it!* In short, I let myself be persuaded.

The assistant came at dawn. We kneaded the loaves, brushed them with seeds, and set them into molds. Then the young man left and I stayed, sitting in the oven pit on a pile of rags. *Well, Gimpl,* I thought, *you've taken revenge for all your suffering.* The frost was crackling outside, but here it was warm. It heated my face. I bent my head and dozed off.

As I fell asleep, Elka appeared in a dream, dressed in her burial shroud, and calling out, "What have you done, Gimpl?"

"It's your fault," I said, and started crying.

She said, "You simpleton! Because Elka is false, is everything a lie? I deceived no one but myself. I'm paying for everything, Gimpl. They spare you nothing here!"

I looked at her face: black as coal. Then I awoke. For a long while I sat silent. I felt like everything hung in the balance. One false step, and I lost the world to come. But God helped me.

I grabbed the oven paddle, pulled out all the loaves, carried them out into the yard, and started digging a ditch in the frozen dirt. In the meantime my young assistant arrived. "Boss," he said, "what are you doing?" And he turned white as a corpse. "It's all right," I said, and buried all the bread before his eyes.

Then I went home, took my stack of money out of its hiding place, and divided it up among the children. "On this night," I said, "I saw your mother. She's having a terrible time." They were stunned and couldn't utter a word. "Be well," I told them, "and forget that there ever was a Gimpl." I put on my coat and a pair of boots. In one hand I took the sack with my prayer shawl, in the other my walking stick—and then I kissed the *mezuzah*. When people saw me in the street, they were completely confused. "Where are you going?" they asked. And I answered, "I'm off into the wide world." And this way I left Frampol.

I wandered throughout the land and was not failed by good people. Years passed. I became old and gray. I heard my fill of tall tales, a lot of lies and inventions, but the longer I lived, the more I saw that there really are no lies.

If it didn't happen to this one, it happened to the next. If not today, then tomorrow, next year, or even next century. What's the difference? More than once, when I heard about some chance event, I thought, *That's impossible*. And then, a year or two later, I heard that it happened somewhere, in a place not unlike Frampol. Even if a tale is invented, there's something to it. Why does one person make up one thing, and a second another?

As I wander from house to house, eating at tables with strangers, I often tell wild tales. About a demon, a magician, a windmill, you name it. The children run around me, "Grandpa, tell us a story." Sometimes they tell me what the story should be about, and I tell it for them. As if I care. Once, a chubby kid told me, "Grandpa, it's all the same story." And as I live, he was right, that little rascal.

It's the same thing with dreams. It's already been so many years since I left Frampol, yet as soon as I close my eyes, I'm there again. And who do you think appears? Elka. She stands by the washbasin, like the day we first met, except her face is glowing, her eyes are shining like the eyes of a pious woman, and she tells me strange things. When I wake up, I forget everything, but meanwhile I feel good. She solves all my problems and it feels like everything is right. I cry out for her and beg her, "Take me with you." And she comforts me, "Be patient, Gimpl. It's nearer than it is far."

She sometimes kisses me, hugs me, cries on my face. And when I wake up I feel her lips and the salty taste of her tears.

Of course the world is a world of lies. But it's one step from the true world. Near the door of the poorhouse where I lie there's a plank for washing the dead. The gravedigger's shovel is ready. The grave is waiting. The worms are hungry. My shroud is ready in my sack. Another beggar is waiting for my straw bed. God willing, when the time comes at last, I'll go there with joy. Whatever may be there, it is all true, without trickery, without mockery or lies. Thank God, there even Gimpl can't be deceived.

Gimpel the Fool

Translated from the Yiddish
by Saul Bellow

ONE

I am Gimpel the fool. I don't think myself a fool. On the contrary. But that's what folks call me. They gave me the name while I was still in school. I had seven names in all: imbecile, donkey, flax-head, dope, glump, ninny, and fool. The last name stuck. What did my foolishness consist of? I was easy to take in. They said, "Gimpel, you know the rabbi's wife has been brought to childbed?" So I skipped school. Well, it turned out to be a lie. How was I supposed to know? She hadn't had a big belly. But I never looked at her belly. Was that really so foolish? The gang laughed and hee-hawed, stomped and danced and chanted a good-night prayer. And instead of the raisins they give when a woman's lying in, they stuffed my hand full of goat turds. I was no weakling. If I slapped someone he'd see all the way to Cracow. But I'm really not a slugger by nature. I think to myself: Let it pass. So they take advantage of me.

I was coming home from school and heard a dog barking. I'm not afraid of dogs, but of course I never want to start up with them. One of them may be mad, and if he bites there's not a Tartar in the world who can help you. So I made tracks. Then I looked around and saw the whole marketplace wild with laughter. It was no dog at all but Wolf-Leib the Thief. How was I supposed to know it was he? It sounded like a howling bitch.

When the pranksters and leg-pullers found that I was easy to fool, every one of them tried his luck with me. "Gimpel, the Czar is coming to Frampol; Gimpel, the moon fell down in Turbeen; Gimpel, little Hodel Furpiece found a treasure behind the bathhouse." And I like a golem believed everyone. In the first place, everything is possible, as it is written in the Wisdom of the Fathers. I've forgotten just how. Second, I had to believe when the whole town came down on me! If I ever dared to say, "Ah, you're kidding!" there was trouble. People got angry. "What do you mean! You want to call everyone a liar?" What was I to do? I believed them, and I hope at least that did them some good.

I was an orphan. My grandfather who brought me up was already bent toward the grave. So they turned me over to a baker, and what a time they gave me there! Every woman or girl who came to bake a batch of noodles had to fool me at least once. "Gimpel, there's a fair in heaven; Gimpel, the rabbi gave birth to a calf in the seventh month; Gimpel, a cow flew over the roof and laid brass eggs." A student from the yeshiva came once to buy a roll, and he said, "You, Gimpel, while you stand here scraping with your baker's shovel the Messiah has come. The dead have arisen." "What do you mean?" I said. "I heard no one blowing the ram's horn!" He said, "Are you deaf?" And all began to cry, "We heard it, we heard!" Then in came Rietze the Candle-dipper and called out in her hoarse voice, "Gimpel, your father and mother have stood up from the grave. They're looking for you."

To tell the truth, I knew very well that nothing of the sort had happened, but all the same, as folks were talking, I threw on my wool vest and went out. Maybe something had happened. What did I stand to lose by looking? Well, what a cat music went up! And then I took a vow to believe nothing more. But that was no go either. They confused me so that I didn't know the big end from the small.

I went to the rabbi to get some advice. He said, "It is written, better to be a fool all your days than for one hour to be evil. You are not a fool. They are the fools. For he who causes his neighbor to feel shame loses Paradise himself." Nevertheless the rabbi's daughter took me in. As I left the rabbinical court she said, "Have you kissed the wall yet?" I said, "No; what for?" She answered, "It's the law; you've got to do it after every visit." Well, there didn't seem to be any harm in it. And she burst out laughing. It was a fine trick. She put one over on me, all right.

I wanted to go off to another town, but then everyone got busy matchmaking, and they were after me so they nearly tore my coattails off. They talked at me and talked until I got water on the ear. She was no chaste maiden, but they told me she was virgin pure. She had a limp, and they said it was deliberate, from coyness. She had a bastard, and they told me the child was her little brother. I cried, "You're wasting your time. I'll never marry that whore." But they said indignantly, "What a way to talk! Aren't you ashamed of yourself? We can take you to the rabbi and have you fined for giving her a bad name." I saw then that I wouldn't escape them so easily and I thought: They're set on making me their butt. But when you're married the husband's the master, and if that's all right with her it's agreeable to me too. Besides, you can't pass through life unscathed, nor expect to.

I went to her clay house, which was built on the sand, and the whole gang, hollering and chorusing, came after me. They acted like bear-baiters. When we came to the well they stopped all the same. They were afraid to start anything with Elka. Her mouth would open as if it were on a hinge, and she had a fierce tongue. I entered the house. Lines were strung from wall to wall and clothes were drying. Barefoot she stood by the tub, doing the wash. She was dressed in a worn hand-me-down gown of plush. She had her hair put up in braids and pinned across her head. It took my breath away, almost, the reek of it all.

Evidently she knew who I was. She took a look at me and said, "Look who's here! He's come, the drip. Grab a seat."

I told her all; I denied nothing. "Tell me the truth," I said, "are you really a virgin, and is that mischievous Yechiel actually your little brother? Don't be deceitful with me, for I'm an orphan."

"I'm an orphan myself," she answered, "and whoever tries to twist you up, may the end of his nose take a twist. But don't let them think they can take advantage of me, I want a dowry of fifty guilders, and let them take up a collection besides. Otherwise they can kiss my you-know-what." She was very plainspoken. I said, "It's the bride and not the groom who gives a dowry." Then she said, "Don't bargain with me. Either a flat 'yes' or a flat 'no'—Go back where you came from."

I thought: No bread will ever be baked from *this* dough. But ours is not a poor town. They consented to everything and proceeded with the wedding.

It so happened that there was a dysentery epidemic at the time. The ceremony was held at the cemetery gates, near the little corpse-washing hut. The fellows got drunk. While the marriage contract was being drawn up I heard the most pious high rabbi ask, "Is the bride a widow or a divorced woman?" And the sexton's wife answered for her, "Both a widow and divorced." It was a black moment for me. But what was I to do, run away from under the marriage canopy?

There was singing and dancing. An old granny danced opposite me, hugging a braided white *challah*. The master of revels made a "God's mercy" in memory of the bride's parents. The schoolboys threw burrs, as on Tishe b'Av fast day. There were a lot of gifts after the sermon: a noodle board, a kneading trough, a bucket, brooms, ladles, household articles galore. Then I took a look and saw two strapping young men carrying a crib. "What do we need this for?" I asked. So they said, "Don't rack your brains about it. It's all right, it'll come in handy." I realized I was going to be rooked. Take it another way though, what did I stand to lose? I reflected: I'll see what comes of it. A whole town can't go altogether crazy.

TWO

At night I came where my wife lay, but she wouldn't let me in. "Say, look here, is this what they married us for?" I said. And she said, "My monthly has come." "But yesterday they took you to the ritual bath, and that's afterward, isn't it supposed to be?" "Today isn't yesterday," said she, "and yesterday's not today. You can beat it if you don't like it." In short, I waited.

Not four months later she was in childbed. The townsfolk hid their laughter with their knuckles. But what could I do? She suffered intolerable pains and clawed at the walls. "Gimpel," she cried, "I'm going. Forgive me!"

The house filled with women. They were boiling pans of water. The screams rose to the welkin.

The thing to do was to go to the House of Prayer to repeat Psalms, and that was what I did.

The townsfolk liked that, all right. I stood in a corner saying Psalms and prayers, and they shook their heads at me. "Pray, pray!" they told me. "Prayer never made any woman pregnant." One of the congregation put a straw to my mouth and said, "Hay for the cows." There was something to that too, by God!

She gave birth to a boy. Friday at the synagogue the sexton stood up before the Ark, pounded on the reading table, and announced, "The wealthy Reb Gimpel invites the congregation to a feast in honor of the birth of a son." The whole House of Prayer rang with laughter. My face was flaming. But there was nothing I could do. After all, I *was* the one responsible for the circumcision honors and rituals.

Half the town came running. You couldn't wedge another soul in. Women brought peppered chickpeas, and there was a keg of beer from the tavern. I ate and drank as much as anyone, and they all congratulated me. Then there was a circumcision, and I named the boy after my father, may he rest in peace. When all were gone and I was left with my wife alone, she thrust her head through the bed-curtain and called me to her.

"Gimpel," said she, "why are you silent? Has your ship gone and sunk?"

"What shall I say?" I answered. "A fine thing you've done to me! If my mother had known of it she'd have died a second time."

She said, "Are you crazy, or what?"

"How can you make such a fool," I said, "of one who should be the lord and master?"

"What's the matter with you?" she said. "What have you taken it into your head to imagine?"

I saw that I must speak bluntly and openly. "Do you think this is the way to use an orphan?" I said. "You have borne a bastard."

She answered, "Drive this foolishness out of your head. The child is yours."

"How can he be mine?" I argued. "He was born seventeen weeks after the wedding."

She told me then that he was premature. I said, "Isn't he a little too premature? She said, she had had a grandmother who carried just as short a time and she resembled this grandmother of hers as one drop of water does another. She swore to it with such oaths that you would have believed a peasant at the fair if he had used them. To tell the plain truth, I didn't believe her; but when I talked it over next day with the schoolmaster he

47

told me that the very same thing had happened to Adam and Eve. Two they went up to bed, and four they descended.

"There isn't a woman in the world who is not the granddaughter of Eve," he said. That was how it was; they argued me dumb. But then, who really knows how such things are?

I began to forget my sorrow. I loved the child madly, and he loved me too. As soon as he saw me he'd wave his little hands and want me to pick him up, and when he was colicky I was the only one who could pacify him. I bought him a little bone teething ring and a little gilded cap. He was forever catching the evil eye from someone, and then I had to run to get one of those abracadabras for him that would get him out of it. I worked like an ox. You know how expenses go up when there's an infant in the house. I don't want to lie about it; I didn't dislike Elka either, for that matter. She swore at me and cursed, and I couldn't get enough of her. What strength she had! One of her looks could rob you of the power of speech. And her orations! Pitch and sulfur, that's what they were full of, and yet somehow also full of charm. I adored her every word. She gave me bloody wounds though.

In the evening I brought her a white loaf as well as a dark one, and also poppy-seed rolls I baked myself. I thieved because of her and swiped everything I could lay my hands on: macaroons, raisins, almonds, cakes.

I hope I may be forgiven for stealing from the Saturday pots the women left to warm in the baker's oven. I would take out scraps of meat, a chunk of pudding, a chicken leg or head, a piece of tripe, whatever I could nip quickly. She ate and became fat and handsome.

I had to sleep away from home all during the week, at the bakery. On Friday nights when I got home she always made an excuse of some sort. Either she had heartburn, or a stitch in the side, or hiccups, or headaches. You know what women's excuses are. I had a bitter time of it. It was rough. To add to it, this little brother of hers, the bastard, was growing bigger. He'd put lumps on me, and when I wanted to hit back she'd open her mouth and curse so powerfully I saw a green haze floating before my eyes. Ten times a day she threatened to divorce me. Another man in my place would have taken French leave and disappeared. But I'm the type that bears it and says nothing. What's one to do? Shoulders are from God, and burdens too.

One night there was a calamity in the bakery: the oven burst, and we almost had a fire. There was nothing to do but go home, so I went home. Let me, I thought, also taste the joy of sleeping in bed in midweek. I didn't want to wake the sleeping mite and tiptoed into the house. Coming in, it seemed to me that I heard not the snoring of one but, as it were, a double snore, one a thin enough snore and the other like the snoring of a slaughtered ox.

Oh, I didn't like that! I didn't like it at all. I went up to the bed, and things suddenly turned black. Next to Elka lay a man's form. Another in my place would have made an uproar, and enough noise to rouse the whole town, but the thought occurred to me that I might wake the child. A little thing like that—why frighten a little swallow, I thought. All right then, I went back to the bakery and stretched out on a sack of flour and till morning I never shut an eye. I shivered as if I had had malaria. "Enough of being a donkey," I said to myself. "Gimpel isn't going to be a sucker all his life. There's a limit even to the foolishness of a fool like Gimpel."

In the morning I went to the rabbi to get advice, and it made a great commotion in the town. They sent the beadle for Elka right away. She came, carrying the child. And what do you think she did? She denied it, denied everything, bone and stone! "He's out of his head," she said. "I know nothing of dreams or divinations." They yelled at her, warned her, hammered on the table, but she stuck to her guns: it was a false accusation, she said.

The butchers and the horse-traders took her part. One of the lads from the slaughterhouse came by and said to me, "We've got our eye on you, you're a marked man." Meanwhile the child started to bear down and soiled itself. In the rabbinical court there was an Ark of the Covenant, and they couldn't allow that, so they sent Elka away.

I said to the rabbi, "What shall I do?"

"You must divorce her at once," said he.

"And what if she refuses?" I asked.

He said, "You must serve a title divorce. That's all you'll have to do."

I said, "Well, all right, Rabbi. Let me think about it."

"There's nothing to think about," said he. "You mustn't remain under the same roof with her."

"And if I want to see the child?" I asked.

"Let her go, the harlot," said he, "and her brood of bastards with her."

The verdict he gave was that I mustn't even cross her threshold—never again, as long as I should live.

During the day it didn't bother me so much. I thought: It was bound to happen, the abscess had to burst. But at night when I stretched out upon the sacks I felt it all very bitterly. A longing took me, for her and for the child. I wanted to be angry, but that's my misfortune exactly, I don't have it in me to be really angry. In the first place—this was how my thoughts went—there's bound to be a slip sometimes. You can't live without errors. Probably that lad who was with her led her on and gave her presents and whatnot, and women are often long on hair and short on sense, and so he got around her. And then since she denies it so, maybe I was only seeing things? Hallucinations do happen. You see a figure or a mannikin or something, but when you come up closer it's nothing, there's not a thing there. And if that's so, I'm doing her an injustice. And when I got so far in my thoughts I started to weep. I sobbed so that I wet the flour where I lay. In the morning I went to the rabbi and told him that I had made a mistake. The rabbi wrote on with his quill, and he said that if that were so he would have to reconsider the whole case. Until he had finished I wasn't to go near my wife, but I might send her bread and money by messenger.

THREE

Nine months passed before all the rabbis could come to an agreement. Letters went back and forth. I hadn't realized that there could be so much erudition about a matter like this.

Meanwhile Elka gave birth to still another child, a girl this time. On the Sabbath I went to the synagogue and invoked a blessing on her. They called me up to the Torah, and I named the child for my mother-in-law—may she rest in peace. The louts and loudmouths of the town who came into the bakery gave me a going-over. All Frampol refreshed its spirits because of my trouble and grief. However, I resolved that I would always believe what I was told. What's the good of *not* believing? Today it's your wife you don't believe; tomorrow it's God Himself you won't take stock in.

By an apprentice who was her neighbor I sent her daily a corn or a wheat loaf, or a piece of pastry, rolls or bagels, or, when I got the chance, a slab of pudding, a slice of honey cake, or wedding strudel—whatever came my way. The apprentice was a good-hearted lad, and more than once he added something on his own. He had formerly annoyed me a lot, plucking my nose and digging me in the ribs, but when he started to be a visitor to my house he became kind and friendly. "Hey, you, Gimpel," he said to me, "you have a very decent little wife and two fine kids. You don't deserve them."

"But the things people say about her," I said.

"Well, they have long tongues," he said, "and nothing to do with them but babble. Ignore it as you ignore the cold of last winter."

One day the rabbi sent for me and said, "Are you certain, Gimpel, that you were wrong about your wife?"

I said, "I'm certain."

"Why, but look here! You yourself saw it."

"It must have been a shadow," I said.

"The shadow of what?"

"Just one of the beams, I think."

"You can go home then. You owe thanks to the Yanover rabbi. He found an obscure reference in Maimonides that favored you."

I seized the rabbi's hand and kissed it.

I wanted to run home immediately. It's no small thing to be separated for so long a time from wife and child. Then I reflected: I'd better go back to work now, and go home in the evening. I said nothing to anyone, although as far as my heart was concerned it was like one of the Holy Days. The women teased and twitted me as they did every day, but my thought was: Go on, with your loose talk. The truth is out, like the oil upon the water. Maimonides says it's right, and therefore it is right!

At night, when I had covered the dough to let it rise, I took my share of bread and a little sack of flour and started homeward. The moon was full and the stars were glistening, something to terrify the soul. I hurried onward, and before me darted a long shadow. It was winter, and a fresh snow had fallen. I had a mind to sing, but it was growing late and I didn't want to wake the householders. Then I felt like whistling, but I remembered that you don't whistle at night because it brings the demons out. So I was silent and walked as fast as I could.

Dogs in the Christian yards barked at me when I passed, but I thought: Bark your teeth out! What are you but mere dogs? Whereas I am a man, the husband of a fine wife, the father of promising children.

As I approached the house my heart started to pound as though it were the heart of a criminal. I felt no fear, but my heart went thump! thump! Well, no drawing back. I quietly lifted the latch and went in. Elka was asleep. I looked at the infant's cradle. The shutter was closed, but the moon forced its way through the cracks. I saw the newborn child's face and loved it as soon as I saw it—immediately—each tiny bone.

Then I came nearer to the bed. And what did I see but the apprentice lying there beside Elka. The moon went out all at once. It was utterly black, and I trembled. My teeth chattered. The bread fell from my hands, and my wife waked and said, "Who is that, ah?"

I muttered, "It's me."

"Gimpel?" she asked. "How come you're here? I thought it was forbidden."

"The rabbi said," I answered and shook as with a fever.

"Listen to me, Gimpel," she said, "go out to the shed and see if the goat's all right. It seems she's been sick." I have forgotten to say that we had a goat. When I heard she was unwell I went into the yard. The nanny goat was a good little creature. I had a nearly human feeling for her.

With hesitant steps I went up to the shed and opened the door. The goat stood there on her four feet. I felt her everywhere, drew her by the horns, examined her udders, and found nothing wrong. She had probably eaten too much bark. "Good night, little goat," I said. "Keep well." And the little beast answered with a "Maa" as though to thank me for the goodwill.

I went back. The apprentice had vanished.

"Where," I asked, "is the lad?"

"What lad?" my wife answered.

"What do you mean?" I said. "The apprentice. You were sleeping with him." "The things I have dreamed this night and the night before," she said, "may they come true and lay you low, body and soul! An evil spirit has taken root in you and dazzles your sight." She screamed out, "You hateful creature! You mooncalf! You spook! You uncouth man! Get out, or I'll scream all Frampol out of bed!"

Before I could move, her brother sprang out from behind the oven and struck me a blow on the back of the head. I thought he had broken my neck. I felt that something about me was deeply wrong, and I said, "Don't make a scandal. All that's needed now is that people should accuse me of raising spooks and *dybbuks*." For that was what she had meant. "No one will touch bread of my baking."

In short, I somehow calmed her.

"Well," she said, "that's enough. Lie down, and be shattered by wheels." Next morning I called the apprentice aside, "Listen here, brother!" I said. And so on and so forth. "What do you say?" He stared at me as though I had dropped from the roof or something.

"I swear," he said, "you'd better go to an herb doctor or some healer. I'm afraid you have a screw loose, but I'll hush it up for you." And that's how the thing stood.

To make a long story short, I lived twenty years with my wife. She bore me six children, four daughters and two sons. All kinds of things happened, but I neither saw nor heard. I believed, and that's all. The rabbi recently said to me, "Belief in itself is beneficial. It is written that a good man lives by his faith."

Suddenly my wife took sick. It began with a trifle, a little growth upon the breast. But she evidently was not destined to live long; she had no years. I spent a fortune on her. I have forgotten to say that by this time I had a bakery of my own and in Frampol was considered to be something of a rich man. Daily the healer came, and every witch doctor in the neighborhood was brought. They decided to use leeches, and after that to try cupping. They even called a doctor from Lublin, but it was too late. Before she died she called me to her bed and said, "Forgive me, Gimpel."

I said, "What is there to forgive? You have been a good and faithful wife."

"Woe, Gimpel!" she said. "It was ugly how I deceived you all these years, I want to go clean to my Maker, and so I have to tell you that the children are not yours."

If I had been clouted on the head with a piece of wood it couldn't have bewildered me more.

"Whose are they?" I asked.

"I don't know," she said. "There were a lot . . . but they're not yours." And as she spoke she tossed her head to the side, her eyes turned glassy, and it was all up with Elka. On her whitened lips there remained a smile.

I imagined that, dead as she was, she was saying, "I deceived Gimpel. That was the meaning of my brief life."

FOUR

One night, when the period of mourning was done, as I lay dreaming on the flour sacks, there came the Spirit of Evil himself and said to me, "Gimpel, why do you sleep?"

I said, "What should I be doing? Eating *kreplach*?"

"The whole world deceives you," he said, "and you ought to deceive the world in your turn."

"How can I deceive the world?" I asked him.

He answered, "You might accumulate a bucket of urine every day and at night pour it into the dough. Let the sages of Frampol eat filth."

"What about the judgment in the world to come?" I said.

"There is no world to come," he said. "They've sold you a bill of goods and talked you into believing you carried a cat in your belly. What nonsense!"

"Well then," I said, "and is there a God?" He answered, "There is no God either." "What," I said, "*is* there then?"

"A thick mire."

He stood before my eyes with a goatish beard and horn, long-toothed, and with a tail. Hearing such words, I wanted to snatch him by the tail, but I tumbled from the flour sacks and nearly broke a rib. Then it happened that I had to answer the call of nature, and, passing, I saw the risen dough, which seemed to say to me, "Do it!" In brief, I let myself be persuaded.

At dawn the apprentice came. We kneaded the bread, scattered caraway seeds on it, and set it to bake. Then the apprentice went away, and I was left sitting in the little trench by the oven, on a pile of rags. Well, Gimpel, I thought, you've revenged yourself on them for all the shame they've put on you. Outside the frost glittered, but it was warm beside the oven. The flames heated my face. I bent my head and fell into a doze.

I saw in a dream, at once, Elka in her shroud. She called to me, "What have you done, Gimpel?"

I said to her, "It's all your fault," and started to cry.

"You fool!" she said. "You fool! Because I was false is everything false too? I never deceived anyone but myself. I'm paying for it all, Gimpel. They spare you nothing here."

I looked at her face. It was black; I was startled and waked, and remained sitting dumb. I sensed that everything hung in the balance. A false step now and I'd lose Eternal Life. But God gave me His help. I seized the long shovel and took out the loaves, carried them into the yard, and started to dig a hole in the frozen earth.

My apprentice came back as I was doing it. "What are you doing, boss?" he said, and grew pale as a corpse.

"I know what I'm doing," I said, and I buried it all before his very eyes.

Then I went home, took my hoard from its hiding place, and divided it among the children. "I saw your mother tonight," I said. "She's turning black, poor thing."

They were so astounded they couldn't speak a word.

"Be well," I said, "and forget that such a one as Gimpel ever existed." I put on my short coat, a pair of boots, took the bag that held my prayer shawl in one hand, my stick in the other, and kissed the *mezuzah*. When people saw me in the street they were greatly surprised.

"Where are you going?" they said.

I answered, "Into the world." And so I departed from Frampol.

I wandered over the land, and good people did not neglect me. After many years I became old and white; I heard a great deal, many lies and falsehoods, but the longer I lived the more I understood that there were really no lies. Whatever doesn't really happen is dreamed at night. It happens to one if it doesn't happen to another, tomorrow if not today, or a century hence if not next year. What difference can it make? Often I heard tales of which I said, "Now this is a thing that cannot happen." But before a year had elapsed I heard that it actually had come to pass somewhere.

Going from place to place, eating at strange tables, it often happens that I spin yarns—improbable things that could never have happened—about devils, magicians, windmills, and the like. The children run after me, calling, "Grandfather, tell us a story." Sometimes they ask for particular stories, and I try to please them. A fat young boy once said to me, "Grandfather, it's the same story you told us before." The little rogue, he was right.

So it is with dreams too. It is many years since I left Frampol, but as soon as I shut my eyes I am there again. And whom do you think I see? Elka. She is standing by the washtub, as at our first encounter, but her face is shining and her eyes are as radiant as the eyes of a saint, and she speaks outlandish words to me, strange things. When I wake I have forgotten it all. But while the dream lasts I am comforted. She answers all my queries, and what comes out is that all is right. I weep and implore, "Let me be with you." And she consoles me and tells me to be patient. The time is nearer than it is far. Sometimes she strokes and kisses me and weeps upon my face. When I awaken I feel her lips and taste the salt of her tears.

No doubt the world is entirely an imaginary world, but it is only once removed from the true world. At the door of the hovel where I lie, there stands the plank on which the dead are taken away. The gravedigger Jew has his spade ready. The grave waits and the worms are hungry; the shrouds are prepared—I carry them in my beggar's sack. Another *schnorrer* is waiting to inherit my bed of straw. When the time comes I will go joyfully. Whatever may be there, it will be real, without complication, without ridicule, without deception. God be praised: there even Gimpel cannot be deceived.

AFTERWORD

Three men got together on an afternoon in the early 1950s to translate a nearly unknown Yiddish story about a Polish-Jewish orphan mocked by his fellow villagers. Two of the men, Irving Howe and Eliezer Greenberg, were established figures in New York's Jewish intellectual world. The third, Saul Bellow, was an emerging star on the American literary scene. The story, published eight years earlier in the special Passover issue of a Zionist Yiddish literary journal, had been written by Isaac Bashevis Singer, who had himself immigrated from Poland almost twenty years earlier. At the time, Singer had released only one novel in English, *The Family Moskat* (1950), an epic about Polish Jewry before the Holocaust, which relatively few people had read.

Howe, Greenberg, and Bellow finished the translation in a few hours and sent it to Philip Rahv at *Partisan Review*, where it was first published in the spring of 1953. A year later, the story appeared in Howe and Greenberg's

65

edited collection *A Treasury of Yiddish Stories*. The title, now canonical, was "Gimpel the Fool," taken from the Yiddish "Gimpl tam," which could be literally rendered as "Gimpl the Simpleton." This series of events is thought to be the breakthrough that brought Singer to the attention of American readers and critics and culminated with the Nobel Prize in 1978. But the history of the story's translation—as well as its composition in Yiddish—suggests that its success was due to factors embedded in the original story.

In revisiting the story's origins, it's important to consider that the translation was done quickly and collaboratively. Howe's version of the events, appearing in *A Margin of Hope* (1982), is that "Bellow had a pretty good command of Yiddish, but not quite enough to do the story on his own. So we sat him down before a typewriter. . . . Lazer [Greenberg] read out the Yiddish sentence by sentence, Saul occasionally asked about refinements of meaning, and I watched in a state of high enchantment. Three or four hours, and it was done. Saul took another half an hour to go over the translation and then, excited, read aloud the version that has since become famous. It was a feat of virtuosity, and we drank a schnapps to celebrate." Considering the actual process of the story's translation, Greenberg should probably have been credited alongside Bellow, but the question of collaboration is not the main problem. The issue is that Bellow, Greenberg, and Howe celebrated their "feat" without considering what Singer—a living author who had been intimately involved in the translation of his first novel into English—might have to say.

The reliability of Howe's account is itself put into doubt by another version of events told by Bellow to Janet Hadda, one of Singer's biographers. Bellow says that Greenberg was the one who approached him about doing the translation, and that Howe was altogether missing. Hadda writes that Bellow "was teaching at Princeton University and finishing his novel, *The Adventures of Augie March*. He simply didn't have the time, he told Greenberg. But Greenberg, undeterred, suggested that he could come to Bellow and read the Yiddish to him; Bellow could translate right onto the typewriter. And so it was." In the Bellovian version, as in Howe's, Greenberg is the only one who *sees* the text before his eyes, which makes Bellow's translation an oral rather than textual performance. Looked at from another perspective, we might say that Bellow translated one of the most important Jewish literary works to appear in the second half of the twentieth century without ever reading the original.

When telling the story of how they translated Singer, both Bellow and Howe mention him in cursory terms. Howe describes his meeting with Singer "several months" later as a lunch in which the Yiddish writer "still entirely unknown to English readers . . . started rolling out a carpet of wisecracks, anecdotes, platitudes, quotations, opinions that left me dizzy with amusement and dismay." In all, Howe does not give the impression of taking Singer seriously, saying that he was either "a genius or a comedian." Bellow's take on Singer, as told to Hadda, was even worse, saying that he was an "opportunist" and a "careerist." Singer was probably a little of all of these—but, as an artist, also much more.

Bellow had projected onto Singer the image of an old-world Yiddish-speaking Jew whom he had carried into American culture. He didn't see Singer as a contemporary writer, but more, as Hana-Wirth Nesher has suggested, as the symbol of an authentic Jewish past lost to the Holocaust. But Bellow did not realize that this symbolic role did not represent Singer as an author. Rather, it was a public persona Singer took on better to fit within his cultural surroundings.

In the years leading up to his publication of "Gimpl tam," Singer's known work in Yiddish consisted of two serially published novels, *Der sotn in Goray* (Satan in Goray, 1933) and *Der zindiker meshiekh* (The sinning messiah, 1935–36), only the first of which was published as a book. He had also authored a few programmatic essays, dozens of stories, and hundreds of articles in the Yiddish press, none of which stood out for its optimism. In 1943, he began publishing a series of stories told from the first-person perspective of the *Yeytser-hore*, the Evil Spirit, a sort of malevolent personage taking on various forms to weave demonic tales. Yet something seems to have changed in 1945, when Singer published two stories—"The Little Shoemakers" and "Simple Gimpl"—which reflected how Jewish tradition could *positively* influence Jewish life in modern times.

The first is more obviously addressed to the plight of what Singer called modern Jews, telling the story of post-Holocaust Jewish renewal in New Jersey. But "Simple Gimpl" was subtler in its address, providing not a story but a myth that would give readers a model for faith in the modern world. Understanding the deliberate nature of "Simple Gimpl" as a modern myth involves delving into the artistic process that shaped its composition—providing a sense of Singer's literary instinct and the way he deployed a web of inputs in writing the story, evinced by his journalistic articles of the time. And the most important influence on this story, as identified by Yiddish scholar David Roskies, is Rabbi Nahman of Bratslav's *Stories of Tales* (1815), which included a story titled "Tale of a Sage and a Simpleton."

Singer had written a series of articles on Rabbi Nahman's life and work as early as December 1939 and January 1940. And he returned to the topic again in April 1944, a year before the publication of "Gimpl tam," focusing on Rabbi Nahman's themes and methods. "This story," writes Singer in one of his articles, "which praises the naive and sincere person of faith, is written in such a folklike, engaging way, that it makes a strong impression—not only on simple readers but also on sophisticated ones. It expresses the deepest truths in the plainest manner, and the story itself is full of suspense, with a kind of magic that only the work of a true artist can possess." A year later, he related folk storytelling directly to modern fiction writing. "The difference between old-time tales and stories by fiction writers today is for the most part that modern fiction writers aim to *represent* characters and their actions. . . . Old-time storytellers and authors did not have this need. They assumed from the outset that readers believed their every word."

Singer's understanding of the role of storytellers in relation to their readers' expectations—and needs—fuses into a single theme: *faith*. Readers need to believe in stories no less than characters need faith to live their fictional lives. And the question of faith and doubt is at the core of Rabbi Nahman's "Tale of a Sage and a Simpleton," in which the sage doubts the existence of the king of the land on the grounds of having never seen him. "It's self-evident," adds Singer, "that, for Rabbi Nahman, the 'king' referred to God, and the 'sage' to the *apikoros*"—a Jewish apostate. The story, he suggests, was written as a tale of faith for the unbelieving Jews of Rabbi Nahman's age.

Bellow was less invested than Singer in old Jewish literary and religious sources, like the tales of Rabbi Nahman, and could never have picked up on the cultural layers informing "Gimpl tam." But Singer, who had lived through the First World War as a teenager, experienced interwar Poland as a young adult, fled to the United States as a refugee, and now stood as a witness to all that was lost as the Second World War ravaged not only his people but also the Jewish way of life in which he had been raised—Singer knew well that the unbelievers of Nahman's days were not the same as those of his own time. On the one hand, he noted in his article that Nahman's story was written in "a folklike, engaging way" that "expresses the deepest truths in the plainest manner." On the other, he saw that the modern American Jews with whom he now lived needed a myth of their own. That myth was "Simple Gimpl."

Like the character of Simple Gimpl, the tale's simplicity is deceptive, and parts of what Bellow and Greenberg missed in the original Yiddish have haunted the story's translation since it first appeared. The first and most important issue has to do with its opening line, which has been discussed in writing at least since Khone Shmeruk raised the issue in 1975. Bellow's version reads, "I am Gimpel the fool. I don't think myself a fool." As has been repeatedly pointed out, the Yiddish original begins, "*Ikh bin Gimpl* tam. *Ikh halt mikh nisht far keyn* nar"—the two emphasized words being different from each other and carrying two different connotations. The first, *tam*, relates to the simple child in the Passover Haggadah, whereas the second, *nar*, relates to someone who is foolish or easily deceived—a distinction discussed in depth elsewhere by Anita Norich. This opening creates tension between faith and deceit, with Gimpl agreeing that he is a simpleton, but not considering himself to be a complete fool.

What is more striking, though, is the degree to which this opening not only *refers* to Rabbi Nahman's tale, but nearly *copies* it word for word. In describing the characters in his story, the narrator in Rabbi Nahman's version refers to one as a *khokhem*, a wise child, and one as a *tam*, adding in Yiddish, "not that he was a *nar*, but his mind was *proste*"—the latter being a Yiddish word for *simple* that comes from Slavic languages. This way, Rabbi Nahman's narrator makes a clear connection between the *tam* and the simpleton.

While slight, Singer's literary tweak to this parenthetical remark was momentous. He took Rabbi Nahman's simpleton and gave him a *voice*. It's one thing for the narrator to make a distinction between simplicity and foolishness on the character's behalf. It's another when the ostensible simpleton makes that distinction himself.

Neither Bellow, nor Greenberg, nor Howe caught this distinction—or many of the other minor elements of the story relating to Jewish tradition and how it might offer some meaning in modern times. One such omission looks, in Bellow's translation, like a throwaway line, but is actually a thread tying together the story's modern and traditional facets. In Bellow's translation, the line reads, "you can't pass through life unscathed, nor expect to." In Yiddish, it reads, *"m'kon dokh nisht shtarbn in laybserdakl."* This could be translated as "You can't, after all, die in ritual undergarments." At first sight, this sentence doesn't appear to make much sense in context, and its full significance is not made clear until the end of the story, when Gimpl—lying on a straw mattress, waiting for death—mentions his *takhrikhim*, or burial shroud, just next to him. In Eastern Europe, Jewish men wore ritual undergarments until they were married, when they received a full-body prayer shawl, usually given as a gift by the bride's family. This fringed garment accompanied them throughout their life during prayer, and was used as their *takhrikhim*. Had Gimpl not married Elka, he would not have had the shroud at hand for burial, which places him within the embrace of Jewish tradition at the moment of death. The sentence does not mean merely that you "can't pass through life unscathed"—it says, quite literally, that you can't die a bachelor, because then you won't have a shroud of your own for burial. No matter how difficult his marriage might have been, just before his death Gimpl reflects on having shared his life with another person. This is the value that Singer puts forth—and problematizes—when this short sentence is considered within the context of the story as a whole.

While researching different aspects of Singer's work at the YIVO Institute for Jewish Research, I came upon a 2006 special issue of the journal *Yiddish*, edited by Joseph Landis, which includes a draft dramatization of "Gimpl tam," prepared by Singer. As I read through the play script, I saw that much of it was a direct English translation of the story made by Singer. In all, this version covered about sixty percent of the text, which meant I was reading what could for all intents and purposes be considered a partial translation by the author. I had done my own translation and started comparing them. When I got to the line mentioned above, I found, "Besides, you can't die a bachelor." They were nearly one-to-one. At that moment, I realized I could create a full version of the story, using my translation to fill out the missing sections, while preserving Singer's authorial voice.

As I did so, I came upon more differences between Singer's and Bellow's versions, all of which shifted the story's tone. At the outset, after Gimpl describes being fooled into thinking that he heard a dog howling, he says that it was actually Wolf Leyb the Thief, adding a phrase that reads "*olev hashnabl*." Language jokes are notoriously difficult to translate, especially one like this, which combines the Germanic and Hebrew aspects of Yiddish, taking the Hebrew phrase *alav ha'sholem*, which means "may he rest in peace," and replaces *sholem* with *shnobl*, which means "nose." This kind of wordplay is so difficult to pull off that Bellow and Greenberg didn't even bother, omitting the phrase completely. Yet in the Singer translation, the phrase is resolved deploying both humor and elegance, with Gimpl saying, "It was Wolf Leyb the Thief, may he rest in pieces." The joke is carried over into the English version—and the wordplay takes place in the target rather than the source language. Singer doesn't translate the joke. He reproduces it in another language. It takes an authorial understanding of both the source language and a command of the target language—as well as a sense of humor that functions in both—to pull off such a solution.

Another interesting phrase appears when Gimpl goes home after being told by the town rabbi that, having retracted his earlier accusations against his wife's infidelity, he is allowed to live with her again. Gimpl leaves the bakery at night, planning to surprise his wife, and walks through the empty village. In Yiddish, looking up at the night sky, he says that the moon was full and that "*di shtern finklen sakones nefoshes.*" The word *shtren* refers to the stars and the phrase *sakones nefoshes* is the Hebrew for mortal danger, but the sentence lacks a clear preposition, so it requires some finessing in English. The solution in Bellow's version is to describe the stars as "glistening, something to terrify the soul," leaving a rather ambiguous impression as to the actual purpose of the image. In Singer's version, the image is clear and vivid: "the stars twinkled as though their lives depended on it." The stars are not there to project fear onto the person walking at night. They are projections of the state of Gimpl's soul. They, like he, sense that life itself is on the line.

Bellow's Gimpel has long been considered an unreliable narrator. Singer's Gimpl, on the other hand, emerges as a more nuanced and complex character—an orphan who, among other things, adopts his wife's illegitimate children and leaves them with an inheritance that he himself never received. From the first words to the last, the ironic tone embedded by Singer in the depths of Gimpl's voice tells an alternative story. Rather than appearing as a fool's tale, it emerges as the deathbed confession of a man who is called simple by others, but who, in reality, is nobody's fool. Gimpl is certainly targeted by his community for ridicule, but his story is ultimately one of self-deception—and of the personal cost of blind faith. He finds redemption from his life of lies only when he does what he had set out to do in the first place: leave Frampol. But instead of starting over in another town, he wanders the world telling stories he knows are untrue, but which he also knows reveal truths we don't yet know. By the end of the story, Gimpl is simple only by name.

"Simple Gimpl" is a modern American invention, devised by Singer to reveal the true foolishness that underlies today's world. In looking at the original alongside the two translations, we see how divergent meanings can emerge from the same words, and how subtle differences can induce different understandings. It also enriches our view of how literature portrays human character by revealing a new Gimpl—one who is less a village dope than a person conflicted yet reconciled with reality, clinging to the only love he had in his life while making peace with the fact that truth and lies sometimes go hand in hand.

—*David Stromberg, Jerusalem*

ABOUT THE AUTHOR, TRANSLATORS, AND ILLUSTRATOR

ISAAC BASHEVIS SINGER (1903–1991) was awarded the Nobel Prize in Literature in 1978. An immigrant from Poland, he arrived in New York in 1935, following in the footsteps of his older brother, Israel Joshua Singer. He produced essays, stories, and other writings for the *Forverts*, often under several pseudonyms. Saul Bellow translated his story "Gimpel the Fool," which heralded his talent for a young generation of American Jewish readers. For years, Singer published his stories in *The New Yorker*, where he developed a distinctive style. His numerous books in English include *Satan in Goray* (1955), *Gimpel the Fool and Other Stories* (1957), *The Magician of Lublin* (1960), *The Slave* (1962), *The Spinoza of Market Street* (1961), *A Friend of Kafka and Other Stories* (1970), *Enemies, a Love Story* (1972), *Old Love and Other Stories* (1979), and *Shadows on the Hudson* (1997). His work has been translated into dozens of languages.

SAUL BELLOW (1915–2005) was born to Russian Jewish parents in Lachine, Quebec, and raised in Chicago. He received his bachelor's degree from Northwestern University in 1937. His novel *The Adventures of Augie March* won the National Book Award for fiction in 1954. Further accolades included the Pulitzer Prize for *Humboldt's Gift* (1975); the Prix International—of which he was the first American recipient—for *Herzog* (1964); and the Croix de Chevalier des Arts et Lettres, the highest literary distinction awarded by the French to non-citizens. In 1976, Bellow was awarded the Nobel Prize in Literature.

DAVID STROMBERG is a writer, translator, and scholar. He is editor of the Isaac Bashevis Singer Literary Trust and recently published an edited collection of Singer's essays, *Old Truths and New Clichés* (2022). His books include *Baddies* (2009), *Idiot Love* (2020), and *A Short Inquiry into the End of the World* (2021), the first novella-length essay in his Mister Investigator series. His second Mister Investigator essay, "The Eternal Hope of the Wandering Jew," was published in 2022 in *The Hedgehog Review*.

LIANA FINCK is a regular contributor to *The New Yorker*, *The Awl*, and *Catapult*. She is a recipient of a Fulbright Fellowship, a New York Foundation for the Arts Fellowship, and a Six Points Fellowship for Emerging Jewish Artists. She has had artist residencies with the MacDowell Colony, Yaddo, the Lower Manhattan Cultural Council, and *Tablet* magazine. Her first book, *A Bintel Brief*, was published in 2014.

RESTLESS BOOKS is an independent, nonprofit publisher devoted to championing essential voices from around the world whose stories speak to us across linguistic and cultural borders. We seek extraordinary international literature for adults and young readers that feeds our restlessness: our hunger for new perspectives, passion for other cultures and languages, and eagerness to explore beyond the confines of the familiar.

Through cultural programming, we aim to celebrate immigrant writing and bring literature to underserved communities. We believe that immigrant stories are a vital component of our cultural consciousness; they help to ensure awareness of our communities, build empathy for our neighbors, and strengthen our democracy.

A B C D E

F G H I J

K L M N O

P Q R S T

U V W X Y

Z

פּעמפּיק: זיידע, ס'איז אַלץ די אייגענע מעשׂה. און כ'לעבן ר'איז גערעכט געווען, דער שייגאַץ.

אַזוי איז דאָס אויך מיט חלומות. שוין אַזוי פֿיל יאָרן ווי כ'בין אַוועק פֿון פֿראַמפּאָל, און ווי נאָר כ'טו זו אַן אויג—בין איך ווידער דאָרט; און וועמען, מיינט איר, זע איך? עלקען. זי שטייט ביי דער באַליע וועש, ווי אין ערשטן טאָג פֿון אונדזער באַגעגעניש, נאָר ס'פּנים שיינט, די אויגן זענען ליכטיק, ווי ביי אַ צדקת, און זי רעדט צו מיר אויסטערלישע רייד. און ווען כ'קום אויף, האָב איך אַלץ פֿאַרגעסן, אָבער דערווייל איז מיר וווּיל. זי פֿאַרענטפֿערט מיר אַלע קשיות און ס'קומט אַרויס אַז אַלץ איז רעכט. כ'וויין פֿאַר איר און בעט איר: נעם מיך צו דיר, און זי טרייסט מיך: האָב געדולד, גימפּל. ס'איז שוין נענטער ווי ווייַטער. צו מאָל קושט זי מיך, האַלדזט מיך, וויינט אויף מיין פּנים, און אַז כ'וועק מיך אויף, שפּיר איך אירע ליפּן און דעם געזאַלצענעם טעם פֿון אירע טרערן.

אוודאי איז די וועלט אַן עולם-השקר, אָבער זי איז איין טריט פֿון דער אמתער וועלט. פֿאַר דער טיר פֿון הקדש, וווּ כ'ליג, שטייט ס'טהרה-ברעט. דער קבֿרות-ייִד האָט גרייט דעם רידל. ס'קבֿר וואַרט. די ווערעם זענען הונגעריק. די תּכריכים ליגן ביי מיר אין דער טאָרבע. אַן אַנדער שנאָרער וואַרט שוין אויף מיין אין בינטל שטרוי. מערטשעשעם, אַז די ציַיט וועט קומען, וועל איך גיין אַהין מיט מיט פֿרייד. וואָס ס'זאָל דאָרט נישט זיַין, אַלץ איז וואָר, אָן פֿאַרדרייעניש, אָן לצנות און שווינדל. גאָט צו דאַנקען: דאָרט קאָן מען אפֿילו גימפּלען אויך נישט אָפּנאַרן.

צווישן די קינדער. כ'האב היינט ביי נאכט, זאג איך, געזען אייער מאמען. זי ווערט נעבעך
גוט פֿארשוואַרצט. זיי זענען געוואָרן אזוי פֿארבליפֿט, אז זיי האָבן נישט געקאָנט קיין ווארט
אריסרעדן. זייט געזונט, זאָג איך צו זיי, און פֿארגעסט, אז ס'איז געווען א מאָל א גימפּל. איך
טו אָן מיין טולוליק, א פֿאַר שטיוול, נעם דעם טלית־זאַק אין איין האַנט, דעם שטעקן—אין
דער אנדערער, און קוש די מזוזה. ווען די לייט האָבן מיך דערזען אין גאַס, זענען זיי שטאַרק
פֿארחידושט געוואָרן.—ווּ גייט איר ערגעץ?—פֿרעגן זיי מיך, און איך ענטפֿער: כ'גיי אין דער
וועלט אריין. און אזוי בין איך אוועק פֿון פֿראַמפּאָל.

איך האָב געוואָגלט איבער דער מדינה און גוטע מענטשן האָבן מיך נישט פֿארלאָזט. יאָרן
זענען אוועק. כ'בין געוואָרן אַלט און גרוי. א סך מעשׂיות האָב איך מיך אָנגעהערט, א סך שקרים
און אויסטראַכטעכצער, אָבער וואָס לענגער כ'האָב געלעבט, אַלץ מער האָב איך איינגעזען, אז
קיין ליגנס זענען גאָרנישט פֿאַראַן. אויב עפּעס געשעט נישט מיט האָצמאַכן, איז מיט גרונעמאַן.
אויב נישט היינט, איז נישט מאָרגן, איבער א יאָר, אָדער גאָר איבער הונדערט יאָר. וואָס איז די
נפֿקא־מינה? נישט איין מאָל, ווען כ'האָב געהערט פֿון א טראַף, האָב איך געקלערט: דאָס קאָן
שוין נישט געמאָלט זיין—און ס'גייט אוועק קיין יאָר אָדער צוויי ווי כ'הער, ס'איז טאַקע ערגעץ
ווו פֿארלאָפֿן. אַפֿילו ווען א מעשׂה איז שוין אויסגעטראַכט, האָט זי אויך א האָפֿט. פֿאַר וואָס
קלערט איינער אויס אזא זאַך און דער צווייטער—אַן אַנדערע?

אזוי ווי כ'גיי איבער די הייַזער און ביי יי פֿרעמדע טישן, קומט מיר אָפֿט אויס צו דערציילן
מעשׂיות—נישט געשטויגן, נישט געפֿלויגן, מיט א שד, א וווילקאָלאַק, א כישוף־מאַכער, א
ווינטמיל, ווייסער וואָס. די קינדער יאָגן מיך ארום: זיידעשי, דערצייַלט א מעשׂה. א מאָל זאָגן
זיי מיר פֿון וואָס צו דערציילן און כ'טו זיי צוליב. א דאַגה האָב איך. איין מאָל זאָגט צו מיר א

כז

באק, מיט לאַנגע ציין און אַ ווײדל. דערהערט אַזוינע ווערטער, האָב איך אים געוואָלט אָנכאַפּן ביַים עק, נאָר כ'האָב מיך אַראָפּגעקוילערט פֿון די זעק מעל און שיער נישט צעבראָכן אַ ריפּ. כ'האָב גראָד געדאַרפֿט טון מײן באַדערפֿעניש און דאָ דערזע איך ס'גרויסע טײג און ס'בעט זיך ממש: טו עס אָפּ. בקיצור, כ'האָב מיך געלאָזט איבעררעדן. פֿאַרטאָג איז געקומען דער געזעל, מיר האָבן אויסגעקנעטן די ברייטלעך, באַשאָטן מיט קימל און אַרײנגעזעצט. דערנאָך איז דער יונג אַוועק און איך בין געבליבן זיצן אין גרוב ביַים אויוון, אויף אַ הויפֿן שמאַטעס. נו, טראַכט איך, האָסט נקמה גענומען, גימפּל, פֿאַר אַלע בזיונות. אין דרויסן האָט געקנאַקט דער פֿראָסט, נאָר דאָ איז געוען וואַרעם. ס'האָט געגליט אין פֿנים. כ'האָב אײנגעבויגן דעם קאָפּ און בין אַנטדרימלט געוואָרן.

ווי כ'שלאָף אײן, קומט מיר צו חלום עלקע, אָנגעטון אין תכריכים, און טוט אַ רוף: וואָס האָסטו אָפּגעטון, גימפּל? זאָג איך: ס'איז אַלץ דײַן שולד, און הייב אָן צו ווײנען. זאָגט זי: דו תם, און אַז עלקע איז פֿאַלש, איז שוין אַלץ פֿאַלש? איך אַלײן האָב אויך קיינעם נישט אָפּגענאַרט אַחוץ מיך אַלײן. כ'צאָל פֿאַר אַלץ, גימפּל; מ'שענקט דאָרט גאָרנישט! כ'טו אַ קוק אויף איר פֿנים: שוואַרץ ווי קויל. באַלד האָב איך מיך אויפֿגעכאַפּט. אַ לאַנגע ווײַל בין איך געבליבן זיצן אַ פֿאַרשטומטער. איך האָב געפֿילט ווי אַלץ הענגט אויף דער וואָגשאָל. אײן טריט—און כ'פֿאַרליר עולם-הבא. אָבער גאָט האָט מיר געהאָלפֿן. כ'האָב אַ כאַפּ געטון די לאָפּעטע, אַרויסגערוקט אַלע לאַבנס, זיי אַרויסגעטראָגן אויפֿן הויף און גענומען גראַבן אַ גרוב אין דער געפֿרוירענער ערד. דערווײַל קומט אָן מײַן יונג. באַלעבאָס, זאָגט ער, וואָס טוט איר? און ער ווערט בלעך ווי אַ מת. ס'איז אַלץ רעכט, זאָג איך, און כ'באַגראָב פֿאַר זײַנע אויגן ס'גאַנצע געבעקס. דערנאָך בין איך אַוועק אַהיים, אַרויסגענומען פֿון באַהעלטעניש ס'פּעקל פּאַפּיר-געלט און צעטיילט

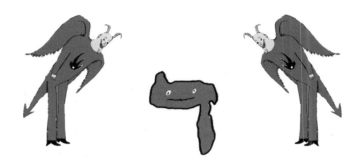

א

יין מאָל בײַ נאַכט, נאָך דער שבעה, ווען כ׳בין געלעגן אויף די זעק און און געדרימלט, איז געקומען צו מיר יענער פאַרשוין, טאַקע דער יצר־הרע אַליין, און זאָגט צו מיר: גימפל, וואָס שלאָפסטו? זאָג איך: וואָס זאָל איך טון? עסן קרעפלעך? זאָגט ער: אַז די גאַנצע וועלט נאַרט דיך, נאַר דו די וועלט. זאָג איך: ווי אַזוי קאָן איך אָפנאַרן אַ וועלט? ענטפערט ער: זאַמל אָן יעדן טאָג אַן עמער השתּנה און בײַ נאַכט טו עס אַריַין אין יוירעכצ. זאָלן זיי, זאָגט ער, פרעסן אומרײנקייט, די פראַמפאָלער חכמים. זאָג איך: וואָס איז מכּח יענער וועלט? זאָגט ער: ס׳איז נישטאָ קיין יענע וועלט. מ׳האָט דיר איַינגערעדט אַ קאָץ אין בויך. זאָג איך, און אַ גאָט איז דאָ? זאָגט ער: ס׳איז קיין גאָט אויך נישטאָ. וואָס זשע, זאָג איך, איז יאָ דאָ? זאָגט ער: אַ טיפע בלאָטע. ער שטייט מיר פאַר די אויגן, דער בעל־דבר: מיט אַ ציגן־בערדל, מיט העֿרנער פון אַ

כה

דיר מוחל צו זײַן? ביסט געווען אַ געטרײַ ווײַב. זאָגט זי: ווײ, גימפּל, כ'האָב דיך נעבעך מיאוס
גענאַרט, אַלע יאָרן. כ'וויל אַוועק צו גאָט ריין. זײַ וויסן, אַז די קינדער זענען נישט דײַנע. וועןן
מ'דערלאַנגט מיר מיט אַ שטאַנג איבערן קאָפּ, וואָלט איך נישט אַזוי צעמישט געוואָרן. וועמענס
זענען זיי?—פֿרעג איך. כ'ווייס נישט', זאָגט זי, ס'זענען געווען אַ סך, נאָר דײַנע זענען זיי נישט.
און אַזוי ווי זי רעדט, טוט זי אַ פֿאַרווואַרף ס'קעפּל, אַ פֿאַרגלאָץ די אויגן און ס'איז אויס עלקע.
אויף די ווײַסע ליפּן איז געבליבן אַ שמייכל. ס'דוכט זיך מיר, אַז זי זאָגט טויטערהייט: כ'האָב
אָפּגענאַרט גימפּלען. דאָס איז געווען דער תכלית פֿון מײַנע פֿאַרשניטענע יאָרן . . .

און כ׳טענה צו איר: מאך ניש׳ ס׳לייטישע געלעכטערטע מער, זאג איך, פֿעלט נישט, נאר מ׳זאל מיר מאכן א שם, אז כ׳האב צו טון מיט יענע לייט. קיינער וועט זיך נישט צורירן צו מיין געבעקס. בקיצור, כ׳האב זי וו ס׳איז איינגעגנומען. נו, א סוף, זאגט זי, לייג דיך און ווער ראדגעבראכן.

צו מארגנס האב איך אוועקגערופֿן דעם געזעל אויף א סודה. הער מיך אויס, ברודער, זאג איך, אזוי און אזוי. וואס זאגסטו? קוקט ער מיך אן וו כ׳וואלט אראפֿגעפֿאלן פֿון דאך. כ׳לעבן, זאגט ער, גיי אריין צו א רופֿא, אדער צו אן אלטער גויע. כ׳האב מורא, זאגט ער, אז ס׳פֿעלט דיר א קלעפֿקע אין קאפֿ. נאר מיין כפרה ביסטו. איכ׳ל קיינעם נישי דערציילן. פתח שין שא. און אזוי איז געבליבן.

צו מאכן א לאנגע מעשׂה קורץ: כ׳האב אפֿגעלעבט מיט מיין ווייב איבער צוואנציק יאר. זעקס קינדערלעך האט זי מיר געהאט: פֿיר מיידלעך און צווי יינגלעך. אין דער צייט האבן פֿאסירט אלערליי זאכן, נאר כ׳האב נישי געזען און נישי געהערט. כ׳האב געגליבט און ווייטער גארנישט. דער רב האט מיר אנומלטן געזאגט: אז דו גלייבסט, איז גלייבסט. ס׳שטייט, אז א צדיק לעבט מיט זיין אמונה.

מיט א מאל איז מיין ווייב שלאף געווארן. אנגעהויבן האט זיך מיט א קליניקייט, א גריזל אויף דער ברוסט. נאר זי האט, א פנים, נישט געהאט קיין יארן. כ׳האב אויסגעגעבן אויף איר א פֿארמעגן. כ׳האב פֿארגעסן צו זאגן, אז כ׳האב שון דעמאלס געהאט א בעקערײַ פֿאר זיך און מ׳האט מיך שון געהאלטן אין פֿראמפֿאל פֿאר א שטיקל נגיד. יעדן טאג איז געקומען דער רופֿא. וו א כישוף־מאכערין, האט מען זי געבראכט צו מיר. מ׳האט געפסלט, געשטעלט פֿיאווקעס, באנקעס. מ׳האט אפֿילו געבראכט א דאקטאר פֿון לובלין, נאר ס׳איז געווען צו שפעט. פֿארן טויט רופֿט זי מיך צו צום בעט און זאגט: גימפל, זיי מיר מוחל. זאג איך: וואס האב איך

כג

גימפּל?—פֿרעגט זי—ווי נעמסטו דיך עפּעס אַהער? . . . דו מעגסט דען? דער רבֿ האָט

געהייסן—ענטפֿער איך און ס'וואַרפֿט מיך ווי אין קדחת. דער מיך אויס, גימפּל, זאָגט זי, גיי

אַרויס אין דרויסן צום קעמערל און גיב אַ קוק צו דער ציג. זי איז, דוכט זיך, חולה. כ'האָב

פֿאַרגעסן צו דערמאַנען, אַז מיר האָבן געהאַט אַ ציג. דערהערט, אַז די קאָזע איז נישט מיט

אַלעמען, גיי איך אַרויס אויפֿן הויף. ס'איז געווען אַ ווייל באַשעפֿעניש. כ'בין צו איר געווען

צוגעבונדן ווי, להבֿדיל, צו אַ מענטש.

כ'גיי צו צום קעמערל מיט שטרויכלענדיקע טריט און עפֿן אויף ס'טירל. די ציג שטייט אויף

די פֿיר פֿיס. כ'טאַפּ זי אַרום, צי זי ביי די הערנער, ריר אָן איר אײַטער. כ'זע נישט קיין שום

שלעכטס. אַוודאי זיך אָנגעפֿרעסן מיט צו פֿיל קאַרע, קלער איך. אַ גוטע נאַכט דיר, קאָזעלע,

זאָג איך, זיי מיר געזונט און שטאַרק. און די שטומע חיה ענטפֿערט מיר אַפֿ מיט אַ מע, אַ

שטייגער ווי זי וואָלט מיר געוואָלט זאָגן אויף שטום-לשון: אַ שיינעם דאַנק.

איך קער זיך אום און זע, אַז דער געזעל איז אויסגערונען. נו, פֿרעג איך, איז דער יונג? וואָס

פֿאַר אַ יונג?—פֿרעגט צוריק מײַן ווייבל. ס'טײַטש. זאָג איך, דער געזעל. ביסט דאָך מיט אים

געשלאָפֿן. וואָס ס'האָט זיך מיר געחלומט די נאַכט און יענע נאַכט, טוט מײַן ווייבל אַ רוף, זאָל

אויסגיין צו דײַן קאָפּ און צו דײַן לײַב און לעבן. נישט אַנדערש, זאָגט זי, נאָר אַ נישט-גוטס האָט

זיך אין דיר באַזעצט און פֿאַרבלענדט דיר די אויגן. זי טוט אַ געשריי: דו נכפהניק, דו מאָנקאַלב,

דו צוריקגעשריגענער, דו קאַלטן, אַרויס פֿון דאַנען, וואָרן כ'על מאַכן אַ געוואַלד, וועט גאַנץ

פֿראַמפּאָל זיך צונויפֿקומען. אײדער וואָס, טוט אַ שפֿרינג אַפֿער איר ברודער פֿון

הינטערן פֿיעקעליק און דערלאַנגט מיר מיט ◼◼◼ ער פֿויסט אַ זעץ גלײַך אין נאָקן אַרײַן. כ'האָב

געמיינט, ר'עט מיר דעם געניק צעברעכן. כ'האָב פֿאַרשטאַנען, אַז עפּעס איז דער מער מיט מיר

בײַ נאַכט, נאָך דעם װי כ׳האָב צוגעדעקט ס׳טייג ס׳זאָל יורן, נעם איך מיר מײַן פּאַרציע
ברויט, שיט אָן אַ זעקעלע מיט געבײַטלט מעל און לאָז מיך גיין אהיים. אין הימל שטײט אַ פֿולע
לבֿנה און די שטערן פֿינקלען סכּנות־נפֿשות. איך שפּאַן און פֿאַרויס לויפֿט אַ לאַנגער שאָטן.
ס׳איז געוואָרן ווינטער און אַ פֿרישער שניי איז געהאַט אָנגעפֿאַלן. מיר וילט זיך זינגען, נאָר ס׳איז
שוין שפּעטלעך און כ׳על נישט גיין אויפֿוועקן די באַלעבאַטים. כ׳וויל פֿײַפֿן, נאָר דאַ דערמאַן
איך מיך, אַז מ׳טאָר נישט פֿײַפֿן קעגן נאַכט צו, ווייל מ׳רופֿט די שדים. שוויייג איך און שפּרייז
אַזוי גיך ווי כ׳קאָן. הײַנט אין די גויישע הײף דערהערן מײַנע טריט און בילן אויף מיר, נאָר איך
קלער מיר: שרײַט אויף די ציין. איר זענט כּלבים און איך בין אַ מענטש, אַ מאַן פֿון אַ לײַטיש
ווײַבל, אַ טאַטע פֿון געראָטענע קינדערלעך.

איך קום צו צו מײַן הײַזל און ס׳האַרץ נעמט מיר קלאַפֿן ווי בײַ אַ גזלן. כ׳האָב נישט קיין
פּחד, נאָר ס׳האַרץ זעצט: בוך, בוך. . . . נו, פֿאַרפֿאַלן. כ׳עפֿן אויף שטילערהייט ס׳קײטל פֿון
דער טיר און קום אַרײַן. עלקע שלאָפֿט שוין. כ׳בלײַב שטיין און טו אַ קוק אויף דער וויג. דער
לאָדן איז פֿאַרמאַכט, אָבער דורך די שפּאַלטן שײַנט אַרײַן די לבֿנה. כ׳זע דאָס קליינע פּנימל
פֿון דעם מיידעלע און כ׳קריג עס גלײַך ליב. אָט אַזוי, מיט איין מאָל. כ׳וואָלט איר שוין געקאָנט
אויסקושן אַלע בײַנדעלעך. דערנאָך דערנענטער איך מיך צום בעט. און וואָס, זע איך
דאָרט? עלקע ליגט און נעבן איר—דער געזעל. די לבֿנה האָט זיך מיט איין מאָל אויסגעלאָשן.
פֿאַר די אויגן איז מיר פֿינצטער חושך. העכט און פֿיס ציטערן מיר פֿויקן.
ס׳ברויט טוט מיר אַ פֿאַל אַרויס פֿון די הענט. ▮▮▮ ווײַב וועקט זיך איבער און פֿרעגט: ווער
איז דאָרט, האַ? . . .

דאָס בין איך—מורמל איך.

אין שכנות, אַ קאָרנברייטל, אַ ווייצנברייטל און אַ מאָל צוגעלייגט אַ שטריצל, אַ פלעצל, אַ
פאַר אייער־בייגעלעך, און אַז ס'האָט זיך גראָד גערעד געמאַכט: אַ שטיקל באַבעלע, אַ פענעץ לעקעך,
אַ קיכל, אַ רעפֿטל פלאָדן, וואָס איז אַרייַנגעפֿאַלן. דער געזעל איז געוון אַ גוטהאַרציקער יונג.
ער האָט אַיר נישט איין מאָל צוגעלייגט געבעקס פֿון זייַן חלק. פֿריִער פלעגט ער זיך טשעפען
צו מיר, מיר שנעלן אין דער נאָז, שטאַרכן אין די זייטן, אָבער זינט ר'איז געוואָרן אָן אייגענער
אין מייַן שטוב, איז ער געוון ווי צו אַ מכה צוצולייגן. העי, דו, גימפל, האָט ער מיר געזאָגט,
האָסט אַ וויל ווייַבל און צוויי פֿאַנע קינדערלעך. ביסט זיי אָסור נישׁ' ווערט. וואָס זאָגסטו דערצו
וואָס לייַט רעדן? —האָב איך אים געפרעגט. מענטשן האָבן לאָנגע צינגער, מאַטלען זיי —האָט
ער געענטפערט —זאָל עס דיך אַרן ווי דער פֿאַריערוקער פֿראָסט.

אין איינעם אַ טאָג האָט דער רבֿ געשיקט נאָך מיר און ער זאָגט: ביסט זיכער, גימפל, אַז
האָסט געהאַט אַ טעות? זאָג איך: אַוודאי, רבי. ס'טײַטש, זאָגט ער, האָסט דאָך אַליין געזען.
ס'האָט געמוזט זייַן אַ שאַטן, זאָג איך. אַ שאַטן, פרעגט ער, פֿון וואָס? און איך ענטפער: פֿון
אַ באַלקן. נו, זאָגט ער, קאָנסט צוריקגייען אַהיים. האָסט אַלץ צו פֿאַרדאַנקען דעם יאַנאָווער
רבֿ. ער האָט געפֿונען אַ פֿאַרוואָרפֿענעם רמב״ם. איך האָב אַ כּף געטאָן דעם רבינס האַנט און
אַ קוש געטאָן. אין אַנהייב האָב איך געוואָלט גלייַך אַהיימלויפֿן. אַ קלייניקייט, מ'זעט נישט אַ
ווייַב און קינדער אַזוי לאַנג. דערנאָך טראַכט איך: איכ׳ל בעסער זיך אומקערן צו דער אַרבעט
און אַהיימגייען ביי נאַכט. איך האָב קיינעם נישט געזאָגט געזאָגט קיין וואָרט, נאָר אין האַרץ איז געוון
יום־טובֿ. די מוידן און די ווייַבלעך האָבן, ווי יעדן טאָג, זיך גערייצט מיט מיר און געמאַכט אויס
מיר ס'געשפעט, נאָר איך טראַכט מיר: רעדט אויפֿגאַרטלדיק. דער אמת איז אַרויס ווי בוימל
אויפֿן וואַסער. אַז דער רמב״ם זאָגט כשר, איז כשר.

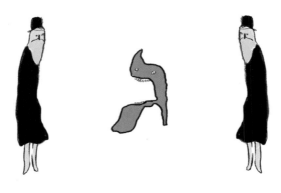

ד

רײַ פֿערטל יאָר האָט געדויערט ביז די רבנים זענען צווישן זיך דורכגעקומען. בריוו
זענען געגאַנגען אַהין און צוריק. כ'האָב נישט געוווּסט, אַז מ'קען לערנען אַזוי פֿיל תּורה וועגן
אַזאַ זאַך. אין דער צײַט האָט עלקע אויסגעטראָגן און געהאַט נאָך אַ קינד. ס'איז דאָס מאָל
געווען אַ מיידל. כ'בין שבת געווען אין שול און געמאַכט דער האַבערין אַ מי־שברך. מ'האָט מיך
אויפֿגערופֿן צום ספֿר און כ'האָב געגעבן אַ נאָמען, נאָר מײַן שוויגער עליה־השלום, די באָדיונגען,
וואָס זענען אַרײַנגעקומען אין דער בעקערײַ, האָבן געהאַט וואָס צו דרעשן מיט די צינגער. גאַנץ
פּראַמפּאַל האָט זיך געקוויקט מיט מײַן שאַנד. אָבער איך האָב בײַ זיך אָפּגעפֿאַסט פֿון הײַנט אָן
אַלץ צו גלייבן. וואָס קומט אַרויס אַז דו גלייבסט נישט? הײַנט גלייבסטו נישׁ' דעם ווײַב, מאָרגן
וועסטו נישט גלייבן אין גאָט. כ'האָב איר יעדן טאָג געשיקט מיט אַ געזעל, וואָס האָט געווענט

און אַז כ'על וועלן זען ס'קינד?—פֿרעג איך. דאַרפֿסט נישט זען ס'קינד, זאָגט דער רבֿ, זאָל זי גייען, די זונה, צוזאַמען מיט אירע ממזרים! ער גיט אַרויס אַ פּסק, אַז כ'טאָר אַפֿילו איר שוועל נישט איבערטרעטן. קיין מאָל נישט. ווי לאַנג כ'על לעבן.

בײַ טאָג האָט עס מיך אַזוי נישט געאַרט. מילא נו, טראַכט איך, דער בלאָטער האָט געמוזט פּלאַצן. אָבער בײַ נאַכט, אַז כ'האָב מיך אַוועקגעלייגט אויף די זעק, איז מיר געוואָרן ביטער. אַ בענקשאַפֿט האָט מיך אָנגעכאַפּט צו איר און צום קינד. כ'האָב געוואָלט זיין אויף איר בײַז, נאָר דאָס איז מיין אומגליק: כ'קאָן נישט זיין בײַז. ערשטנס, טראַכט איך, מאַלע אַ מענטש באַנאַרישט זיך. מסתּמא האָט זי דער יונגאַטש געמאַכט צו איר אַן אייגל, אפֿשר איר געגעבן אַ מתּנה, און אַ נקבֿה האָט לאַנגע האָר און אַ קורצן שׂכל, האָט ער זי איבערגערעדט. צווייטנס, אַז זי לייקנט אַזוי, אפֿשר איז עס געווען אַ פֿאַרבלענדעניש? ס'טרעפֿט אַ מאָל, מ'זעט עפּעס אַ געשטאַלט, צי אַ מענטשעלע, נאָר אַז קומסט צו נאָענט, לאָזט זיך אויס אַ טײַך. אויב אַזוי, געשעט דאָך איר אַן עוולה. ווי כ'טראַכט אַזוי, הייב איך אָן צו ווײַנען. כ'האָב אַזוי געהעשעט, אַז ס'מעל איז נאַס געוואָרן. צו מאָרגנס אין דער פֿרי בין איך אַוועק צום רבֿ און געזאָגט, אַז כ'האָב געהאַט אַ טעות. דער רבֿ האָט פֿאַרשריבן מיט אַ געגדזענער פּען און געענטפֿערט, אַז ער וועט שיקן אַ שאלת־תּשובֿה. ביז דעמאָלס טאָר איך מיך צום ווײַב נישט דערנענטערן. אָבער כ'האָב געמעגט איר שיקן מיט אַ שליח געבעקס און געלט אויף איר אויסקומעניש.

אויף די שפּיץ פֿינגער. כ'קום אַרײַן אין מײַן שטיבל און עפּעס הער איך אַ טאַפּלט שנאָרכן.
אײַן שנאָרך אַ דינער און דער אַנדערער—ווי פֿון אַ געקוילעטן אָקס. די מעשׂה איז באַלד
נישט געפֿעלן. כ'גיי צו צום בעט און ס'ווערט מיר פֿינצטער אין פּופֿיק: נעבן עלקען ליגט אַ
מאַנסביל. אַן אַנדערער אויף מײַן אָרט וואָלט געמאַכט אַ געשריי, אַז אַ האַלבע שטאָט וואָלט
זיך צונויפֿגעלאָפֿן; אָבער איך האָב געטראַכט: צו וואָס איבערוועקן ס'קינד? וואָס איז דאָס
שוועלבעלע נעבעך שולדיק? מילא, כ'בין צוריק אַוועק אין דער בעקערײַ און זיך אַוועקגעלייגט
אויף די זעק מעל. כ'האָב ביז פֿאַרטאָג נישט געקאָנט קיין אויג צוטון. ס'האָט מיך געוואָרפֿן
ווי אין קדחת. גענוג, טראַכט איך, געוווען אַן אײַזל. גימפּל וועט זיך מער נישט לאָזן אָנפֿײַפֿן אַן
אויער. צו גימפּלס נאַרישקייטן איז דאָ אויך דאָ אַ גרענעץ.

אין דער פֿרי בין איך אַוועק צום רב פֿרעגן אַ שאלה. אין שטעטל איז געוואָרן אַ הַאַרמי-
דער. מ'האָט גלײַך געשיקט נאָך אַיר דעם שמש. מײַן ווײַב איז געקומען מיטן קינדעלע אויף די
הענט. און וואָס, מיינט איר, האָט זי געטאָן? געלייקנט שטיין און ביין. ר'איך, זאָגט זי, פֿון זינען
אַראָפּ. כ'ווייס נישט פֿון קיין פּתרון און פֿון קיין חלום. מ'האָט אויף איר געשריגן, זי געוואָרנט,
געקלאַפּט אין טיש, נאָר זי בלײַבט בײַם זיך איריקן: מ'מאַכט אויף איר אַ פֿאַלשן בלבול. די קצבֿים
און די פֿערדהענדלער האָבן זיך געשטעלט אויף איר צד. אַ קײַלער יונג קומט צו מיר צו און
זאָגט מיר: ביסט בײַ אונדז אַ געצעטלטער. דערווײַל האָט ס'קינד זיך גענומען רײַסן און זיך
נעבעך אײַנגעריכט. אין בית-דין-שטוב איז געשטאַנען אַן אָרון-קודש און מ'האָט זי אַוועקגעשיקט.

איך זאָג צום רבין: וואָס זאָל איך טון? זאָגט ער: מוזסט זי באַלד גטן. און אַז זי'ט נישט נעמען
קיין גט? פֿרעג איך. זאָגט ער: וועסטו איר אָנהענגען. זאָג איך: גוט, רבי, כ'על מיך איבערקלערן.
ס'איז נישטאָ וואָס צו קלערן, זאָגט דער רב, טאָרסט מיט איר נישט זײַן אונטער איין באַלקן.

וואָרט. זי קריכט דיר אַרײַן אין דער זיבעטער ריפ און דו ליגסט אויפֿן פּיעקעליק אין געהאַקטע
ווענדן און ווילסט נאָר. עלעהיי אַ געבראָטנס. אין אָוונט האָב איך איר אַחוץ געבראַכט
אַ חלה, וואָס איך האָב אײגנס אָפּגעבאַקן פֿאַר אירעט וועגן, און אַ פֿאַר זעמעלעך. כ'בין צוליב
איר געוואָרן אַ גנבֿ און געלקחנט וואָס איך האָב נאָר געקענט: דאָ אַ שטיקל קוכן און דאָרט אַ
מאַקאַראַנדל, פֿון דאַנען אַ ראָזשינקע און פֿון דאָרט אַ מאַנדל. ס'זאָל מיר צו קיין גנאַי נישט זײַן:
כ'פֿלעג עפֿענען שבת טשאָלנטער און אַרויסנעמען אַ פֿאַדעם פֿלייש, אַ פּיצל קוגל, אַ קעפּל, אַ
פֿיסל, אַ שטיקל קישקע, וואָס ס'האָט זיך געלאָזט. זי האָט געגעסן און געוואָרן שיין און פֿעט.
אַ גאַנצע וואָך האָב איך נישט געגעסן גענעכטיקט אין דער היים. פֿרײַטאָג צו נאַכט פֿלעג איך קומען
צו איר, נאָר זי האָט זי אַלע מאָל געהאַט אַן אויסרייד. דאָ האָט איר געברענט אונטערן לעפֿעלע
און דאָ האָט זי געשטאָכן אין דער זײַט; דאָ האָט זי געהאַט אַ שלוקעכץ און דאָ אַ קאָפּווייטאָג.
הײַנט די ווײַבערשע שאלות! פֿרעגט נישט, כ'בין אויסגעריסן געוואָרן. דערצו איז דער ברודער
אירער, דער ממזר, אונטערגעוואַקסן. ער האָט מיך געשלאָגן און אַז איך האָב געוואָלט צוריק
טון האָט זי דערלאַנגט אַ מענה-לשון, אַז ס'איז מיר גרין געוואָרן פֿאַר די אויגן. צען מאָל אין
טאָג האָט זי מיר געוואָרפֿן דעם גט פֿאַר די פֿיס. אַן אַנדערער אויף מײַן אָרט וואָלט אַנטלאָפֿן
ווי דער שוואַרצער פֿעפֿער וואַקסט; אָבער איך בין בטבֿע אַ פֿאַרשווײַגער. נו, הכלל, וואָס זאָל
מען טון? אַז גאָט גיט פּלײַצעס מוז מען שלעפּן דעם פּאַק.

אין איינער אַ נאַכט האָט געטראָפֿן אין דער בעקערײַ אַ צרה: דער אויוון האָט געפּלאַצט
און ס'איז שיער נישט געוואָרן אַ שׂרפֿה. אַזוי ווי כ'האָב נישט געהאַט וואָס צו טון, בין איך
מיר אַוועק אַהיים. לאָמיך, טראַכט איך, אויך אַ מאָל פֿאַרזוכן דעם טעם פֿון שלאָפֿן אין בעט
אין אַ מיטן מיטוואָך. כ'האָב נישט געוואָלט אויפֿוועקן ס'פּיצעלע און בין אַרײַן אין דער שטיל,

טענה איך, אַז האָסט עס געהאַט זיבעצן וואָכן נאָך דער חתונה? דערצייילט זי מיר אַ מעשׂה,
אַז ס'איז אַ זיבעלע. זאָג איך, אַ זיבעלע איז נישט קיין פֿינפֿטל. נעמט זי טענהן, באַשר זי האָט
געהאַט אַ באָבען, האָט זי אין גאַנצן געטראָגן פֿינף חדשים און זי געראָטן אין איר אַריין וו צוויי
טראָפֿנס וואַסער. זי שוואָרט דערבייַ מיט אַזוינע שבֿועות, אַז מ'וואָלט געקאָנט גלייבן אַ גוי אויפֿן
יאָריד. דעם אמת געזאָגט, האָב איך נישט געגלייבט; אָבער אַז כ'האָב מאָרגן איבערגערעדט
מיט אַ מלמד, האָט ער מיר געזאָגט אַז אַזאַ זאַך ווערט געבראַכט אין דער גמרא. אָדם און חוה
זענען אַרויף אויפֿן בעט צוויי און אַראָפּ זענען זיי פֿיר. נו, זאָגט ער, יעדע אשה איז דער מוטער
חוה אַן אוראייניקל, און וואָס איז אים עלקע ערגער פֿון חוה'ן? אַזוי צי אַזוי, מ'האָט מיר פֿאַרערעדט
די ציין. און צוריקגעשמועסט, ווער ווייסט? אָט זאָגט מען דאָך, ס'יויזל האָט אין גאַנצן קיין
טאָטן נישט געהאַט.

כ'האָב שוין אָנגעהויבן פֿאַרגעסן מייַן בראָך. כ'האָב ליב געהאַט ס'קינד אַ געוואַלד און ער
האָט מיך אויך ליב געהאַט. וווּ נאָר ר'האָט מיך דערזען, אַזוי האָט ער אָנגעהויבן מאַכן מיט די
הענטעלעך, כ'זאָל אים נעמען. אַז ר'האָט זיך גערייסן אָדער זיך פֿאַרקייכט, האָט אים קיינער נישט
געקאָנט איינשטילן אַחוץ מיר. כ'האָב אים געקויפֿט אַ ביינערן ביַיגעלע, אַ קאַפֿעלע געליישט
מיט גאָלד. יעדן מאָנטיק און דאָנערשטיק האָט מען אים געטאָן אַ בייַ אויג און כ'בין געלאָפֿן
אָפּשפּרעכן. געאַרבעט האָב איך דעמאָלס ווי אַן אָקס. אַז ס'איז דאָ אַן עופֿעלע אין הויז, איז
ס'באַדערפֿעניש גרעסער. הלמאַי זאָל איך ליגן זאָגן? כ'האָב זי, עלקען, אויך נישט פֿייַנט. זי
האָט מיך געזידלט און געשאָלטן און איך בין געקראָכן אונטער די נעגל. אוי, האָט זי געהאַט
אַ כּוח! אַז זי האָט אויף דיר אַ קוק געטאָן מיט איר קוקעלע, ביסטו געוואָרן אַ געפּלעפֿטער.
הײַנט איר רייידעלעך! זי שיט מיט פֿעך און שוועבל און ס'איז מלא־חן, אויסצוקושן יעדעס

יונגען נישט געדאַרפֿט. איך בין געשטאַנען אין אַ ווינקל און געבעטן גאָט, און זיי האָבן אויף
מיר געשאָקלט מיט די קעפּ. זאָג, האָבן זיי מיר אונטערגעגעבן חשק, פֿון זאָגן ווערט מען ניש'
טראַגן. איינער אַ שנעק האָט מיר דערלאַנגט אַ שטריווש צום מויל: אַ בהמה דאַרף עסן שטרוי.
כ'לעבן, ר'איז גערעכט געווען אויך.

זי איז צו מזל געלעגן געוואָרן און געהאַט אַ בן-זכר. פֿרײַטאָג צו נאַכט טוט דער שמשׂ אַ
שפּאַן אַרויף אויפֿן באַלעמער, דערלאַנגט אַ קלאַפּ אין שולחן און רופֿט אויס: הנגיד ר' גימפּל
פֿאַרבעט דעם גאַנצן עולם אויף אַ שלום-זכר. ס'גאַנצע בית-מדרש האָט געלאַכט. ס'פּנים איז מיר
פֿאַרפֿאַטשעט געוואָרן. אָבער וואָס האָב איך געקענט טון? כ'בין פֿאָרט געווען דער בעל-ברית.
ס'איז זיך אָנגעלאָפֿן אַ האַלבע שטאָט. מ'האָט קיין שפּילקע געקאָנט אַרײַנשטעקן. ווײַבער
האָבן געבראַכט געפֿעפֿערטע אַרבעס און מ'האָט געקריגן פֿון שענק אַ פֿעסעלע ביר. כ'האָב
געגעסן און געטרונקען גלײַך מיט אַלעמען און מ'האָט מיר געוווּנטשן מזל-טובֿ. דערנאָך האָט
מען געמאַכט אַ ברית און כ'האָב אַ נאָמען געטון דעם יונגל נאָך מײַן טאַטן עליו-השלום. אַז
אַלע זענען אַוועק און איך בין געבליבן מיט דער געוויינערין אַליין, האָט זי אַרויסגעשטעקט דעם
קאָפּ פֿון פֿאַרהאַנג און מיך צוגערופֿן צום בעט. גימפּל, זאָגט זי, וואָס שווײַגסטו? אַ שיף מיט
זויערמילך איז דיר אונטערגעגאַנגען? וואָס זאָל איך רעדן, זאָג איך, שיין האָסטו מיר אָפּגעטון.
ווען מײַן מאַמע וואָלט דאָס דערלעבט, וואָלט זי נאָך אַ מאָל געשטאַרבן. זאָגט זי: ביסט מטורף
אָדער וואָס? ס'טײַטש? כ'האָג איך, זאָג איך, ווי מאַכט מען דאָס אַ מאַנסביל אַזוי צום נאַר? וואָס טוט זיך
מיט דיר? פֿרעגט זי. וואָס האָסטו דיר אַרײַנגענומען אין קאָפּ אַרײַן? כ'האָב געזען, אַז כ'מוז
מיט איר רעדן אָפֿענע דיבורים, זאָג איך: אַזוי טוט מען מיט אַ יתום? אַ ממזר האָסטו געבוירן.
זאָגט זי: שלאָג דיר אַרויס פֿון זין די נאַרישקייטן. ס'איז דײַן קינד. ווי אַזוי איז דאָס מײַן קינד,

ב

יי נאַכט בין איך געקומען צום וויבס געלעגער, אָבער זי לאָזט מיך נישט אַרײַן.

ס׳טײַטש, זאָג איך, דערויף האָבן מיר חתונה געהאַט? זאָגט זי: כ׳בין טריף געוואָרן. ס׳הייסט,

טענה איך, מ׳האָט דאָך ערשט נעכטן דיך געפֿירט מיט כלי־זמר אין מקוה אַרײַן. זאָגט זי: הײַנט

איז ניש׳ נעכטן און נעכטן איז ניש׳ הײַנט. אויב ס׳געפֿעלט דיר נישט, נעם ס׳פּעקל. בקיצור,

כ׳האָב געוואָרט. ס׳גייט נישט אַוועק פֿיר חדשים און מײַנע נעמט גיין צו קינד. גאָנץ פֿראָמפֿאָל

האָט געלאַכט אין די פֿויסטן אַרײַן, אָבער וואָס האָב איך געקאָנט טון? זי איז פֿאָרט געלעגן

אין יסורים. זי האָט געריסן די וועגט. גימפּל, שרײַט זי, כ׳בין פֿאַרבײַ. זײַ מיר מוחל! די שטוב

איז געוואָרן פֿול מיט וויבער. מ׳האָט געקאָכט טעפּ וואַסער, ווי צו טהרה. די געוואַלדן זענען

געגאַנגען צום הימל. הכּלל, כ׳בין אַוועק אין בית־מדרש זאָגן תהילים. מער האָבן די ווילע

אויס דיר חזק, דעם זאָל אָנוואַקסן אַ חזק אויף דער נאָז. נאָר זאָל ק"קעלע-קהל נישט מיינען,
אַז מ'קאָן אין מיר האָבן ס'גענאַר. איך וויל, זאָגט זי, פופציק גילדן נדן און אַן אויסשטייער. ווען
נישט, קאָנען זיי מיר קושן אין ווי-הייסט-מען-עס. (זי'ט גערעדט געמיינע רייד). זאָג איך: נדן
גיט דאָך די כלה, נישט דער חתן. זאָגט זי: דינג דיך ניש' מיט מיר. יאָ—יאָ, ניין—ניין, גיי פֿון
וואַנען ביסט געקומען. כ'האָב שוין געמיינט, אַז ס'עט פֿון דעם טייג קיין ברויט נישט זיין, אָבער
ס'איז נישטאָ קיין אָרעם קהל. מ'האָט איר אַלץ נאָכגעגעבן און מ'האָט געמאַכט אַ חתונה.
ס'איז גראָד געווען אַן אונטערגאַנג פֿון לאַקיסרעכץ און די חופה האָט מען געשטעלט אויפֿן
בית-עולם נעבן טהרה-שטיבל. די חברה-לייט האָבן זיך אָנגעשיכורט. ביים שרייבן די כתובה הער
איך וי דער רב דער פרעגט: איז די כלה אַ גרושה, אָדער אַן אלמנה? ביידע, ענטפֿערט די גבאיטע.
ס'איז מיר געוואָרן פֿינצטער אין די אויגן, אָבער וואָס האָב איך געקאָנט טון? אַנטלויפֿן פֿון
אונטער דער חופה? מ'האָט אָפּגעשפילט און אָפּגעטאַנצט. אַ באַבע האָט מיר אַקעגנגעטאַנצט
מיט אַ קוילעטש. דער בדחן האָט געמאַכט אַן אל-מלא-רחמים. חדר-יינגלער האָבן געוואָרפֿן
שטעכלקעס, ווי תשעה-באָב. ס'איז געפֿאַלן אַ סך דרשה-געשאַנק: אַ לאָקשנברעט, אַ מולטער,
אַ שאָף, אַ בעזעמער, קאָכלעפֿל, אַ גאַנצע באַלעבאַטישקייט. כ'טו אַ קוק: צוויי יונגען טראָגן
אַ וויג. וואָס עפּעס אַ וויג? פֿרעג איך. זאָגט מען מיר: זאָל דיר דער קאָפ נישט דאַרן. ס'איז
רעכט. ס'עט צו נוץ קומען. כ'האָב שוין געזען, אַז מ'האָט מיך געפֿירט אין באָד אַריין. אָבער
צוריקגעשמועסט, וואָס האָב איך דאָ פֿאַרלוירן? כ'האָב מיר געקלערט; כ'על אָפּוואַרטן און זען
ס'גרייטע. אַ גאַנצע שטאָט איז דאָך נישט משוגע.

וואָסער אין אויער. זי איז געווען אַ וויבל, האָט מען מיר איינגערעדט, אַז זי איז אַ מויד. זי האָט
געהונגקען אויף אַ פֿוס, האָט מען מיר איינגעשמועסט, אַז זי מאַכט זיך אַזוי, פֿון שיינקייט וועגן. זי
האָט געהאַט אַ ממזר, האָבן זיי געזאָגט, אַז ס'איז אַ יינגערער ברודער. כ'האָב געשריגן: אומזיסט
אַיערע רייד. כ'על מיט דער הור צו דער חופה נישׁ' גיין. האָבן זיי געטענהט: אַז דו רעדסט שוין
יאָ אַזוי שיין, וועט מען דיך נעמען צום רב און וועסט צאָלן קנס, וויל האָסט געמאַכט אַ שם
אַ ייֿדישער טאָכטער. כ'האָב געזען, אַז כ'על שוין קיין גאַנצער פֿון זייערע הענט נישׁט אַרויס,
טראַכט איך: מיַין כפרה איז עס. איך בין דער מאַנסביל, נישׁט זי. אויב ס'איז איר ליב, איז מיר
ניחא. צווייטנס, מ'קאָן דאָך נישׁט שטאַרבן אין לייבסערדאַקל. כ'בין אַוועק צו איר אין ליימענעם
הייזל אויפֿן זאַמד, און די גאַנצע קאַפעליע איז מיר נאָכגעגאַנגען, ווי אַ בערך-טרייבער. ווען מ'איז
צוגעקומען צום ברונעם, האָבן זיי זיך פֿונדעסטוועגן אָפגעשטעלט. מיט עלקען האָבן זיי מורא
געהאַט אָנצוהייבן. זי האָט געהאַט אַ מיַילכל ווי אויף שרויפֿן. כ'בין אַריַין אינעווייניק. ס'גאַנצע
הויז איז געווען אַ שטיבל אָן אַ בריק. פֿון וואַנט צו וואַנט זענען געווען פֿאַרצויגן שטריק און
ס'האָט זיך געטריקנט וועש. זי איז געשטאַנען אַ באָרוועסע ביַי דער באַליע און געוואַשן גרעט.
אָנגעטון איז זי געווען אין אַ באַרכעטן קלײדל. זי האָט געהאַט צווײ צעפעלעך, ווי, להבֿדיל, אַ
שיקסע, פֿאַרדרייט אין ביידע זיַיטן אין קרענצלעך. ס'האָט מיר אַזש פֿאַרכאַפט דעם אָטעם. זי
האָט שוין, אַ פנים, געוווסט ווער כ'בין, ווײל זי טוט אויף מיר אַ קוק און זאָגט:

‏–ס'קאַצל קומט, ר'איז דאָך דאָ, דער יאָלד. נעם אַ בענקל און ווער צעזעצט.

כ'האָב איר אַלץ געזאָגט, גאָרנישׁט געליײקנט. זאָג מיר דעם אמת, זאָג איך, ביסטו אויף
דער וואָר אַ בתולה און איז טאַקע דער יונג יחיאל מזיק דיַין ברודערל? מאַך נישׁ' אויס מיר
קיין חוזק, זאָג איך, ווײַל כ'בין אַ יתום. כ'בין אויך אַ יתומה, ענטפֿערט זי, און ווער ס'מאַכט

טריקעגנען א בלער פֿארפֿל, האָט מיך געמוזט איין מאָל אָפּנאַרן. גימפּל, אויפֿן הימל איז
א יאריד. גימפּל, דער רבֿ האָט זיך אָפּגעקעלבט און געהאַט א זיבעלע. א קו איז געפֿלויגן איבערן
דאַך און געלייגט מעשענע אייער. א מאָל קומט א ישיבֿה־בחור קויפֿן א פֿלאַמפֿלעצל און ער טוט
א זאָג: דו, גימפּל, שארסט מיט דער לאָפּעטע און דרויסן איז געקומען משיח, ס׳איז תחית־המתים.
ס׳טייטש, זאָג איך, מ׳האָט דאָך נישט געהערט בלאָזן שופֿר. זאָגט ער: ביסט טויבֿ? און אלע נעמען
שרײַען: מיר׳ן געהערט, געהערט. אזוי ווי ער רעדט קומט רײַצע די ליכטציערין און טוט א רוף מיט
איר הייזעריק קול: גימפּל, דײַנע טאַטע־מאַמע זענען אויפֿגעשטאנענ פֿון קבֿר. זיי זוכן דיך ארום.
הלמאַי זאָל איך זאָגן, כ׳האָב גאנץ גוט געוווּסט, אז ס׳איז נישט געשטויגן נישט געפֿלויגן, אָבער
פֿארט, מענטשן רעדן. כ׳האָב אָנגעטון דעם שפּענצער און גיי ארויס. אפֿשר יאָ. וואָס פֿארליר
איך דערפֿון? נו־נו, האָט מען מיר געמאַכט א קאָצן־מוזיק מיט א פּעקל. כ׳האָב געטאָן א נדר מער
גארנישט צו גלייבן. האָט ווידער נישט געטויגט. מ׳האָט מיך אזוי צעמישט, אז כ׳האָב שוין נישט
געוווּסט ווו איין און ווו אויס. כ׳בין אוועק צום רבֿ פֿרעגן אן עצה. זאָגט ער: ס׳טייטש, בעסער
זײַ א שוטה אלע יאָרן איידער איין שעה א רשע. דו ביסט, זאָגט ער, נישׂ קיין נאַר. די נאראָנים
זענען זיי, ווײַל אז מ׳פֿארשעמט דעם אנדערן, פֿארלירט מען יענע וועלט. פֿונדעסטוועגן האָט מיך
דעם רבֿס טאָכטער אָפּגענאַרט. אז כ׳בין ארויס פֿון בית־דין־שטוב, זאָגט זי: האָסט שוין געקושט
די וואַנט? זאָג איך: ניין. צו וואָס? זאָגט זי: ס׳איז דאָ אזאַ דין, אז מ׳קומט צום רבֿ, קושט מען די
וואַנט. נו, מיינסט האַלבן, האָב איך געטאָן א קוש אין בײַשטידל. ס׳קאַסט מיך טײַער? און זי טוט
א בעטש ארויס מיט א געלעכטער. באוויזן א קונץ און געלײַזט בײַ גימפּלען.

כ׳האָב שוין געוואָלט אוועק אין אן אנדער שטאַט, אָבער דערווײַל האָט דער עולם מיר
גענומען רעדן א שידוך. ס׳הייסט גערעדט? מ׳האָט מיר די פֿאָלעס אָפּגעריסן. כ׳האָב געקריגן א

דריי דיך, אַנשטאַט ראָזשינקעס, וואָס מ'טיילט ביַי אַ קימפּעטטאָרין, האָט מען מיר אַריַינגעשטופּט אַ הויפֿן ציגן־באָבקעס. ווי איר קוקט מיך אָן בין איך נישט געוואָרן קיין מלופּם־קינד. אַז איך האָב דערלאַנגט אַ פּאַטש האָט מען געזען קראַקע. אָבער כ'בין בטבֿע נישט קיין שלעגער. כ'טראַכט: זאָל מיַינס איבערגיין. דעריבער האָט מען אין מיר אַ קונה.

כ'בין געגאַנגען פֿון חדר און הער ווי אַ הונט בילט. כ'האָב נישט קיין מורא פֿאַר קיין הינט, אָבער כ'וויל נישט אָנהייבן מיט קיין כּלבֿ. ער קאָן אַ מאָל זיַין משוגע און אַז ער טוט דיר אַ ביס, וועט דיר קיין טאַטער נישט העלפֿן. נו, האָב איך געמאַכט פֿיס. כ'טו אַ קוק: דער גאָנצער מאַרק קוילערט זיך פֿון געלעכטער. ס'איז נישט געוואָרן קיין הונט, נאָר וואָלף־לייב גנבֿ עליו השנאַבל. ווי האָב איך דאָס געקאָנט וויסן? אַז ר'האָט פֿאַרט געהוילט ווי אַ צוויג.

אַז די עכברושים האָבן דערשמעקט, אַז כ'זאָל מיך נאַרן, האָט יעדער איינער געפֿרווּוט ס'מזל. גימפּל, דער קייסער קומט קיין פֿראַמפּאָל; גימפּל, גימפּל, די לבֿנה איז אַראָפּגעפֿאַלן אין טורבין; גימפּל, האָדעלע שמויש האָט געפֿונען אַן אוצר הינטערן באָד. און איך, גולם, האָב געגלייבט. וואַרעם ערשטנס קאָן אַלץ טרעפֿן, ווי ס'שטייט אין פּרק, כ'געדענק שוין נישט ווי אַזוי. צווייטנס האָב איך שוין געמוזט גלייבן. אַז גאַנץ קהל פֿאַרלייגט זיך אויף אַ מענטש! טאָמער האָב איך אַ מאָל געפֿרווּוט זאָגן: ע, ס'איז צופֿליַיסנס, איז געוואָרן אַ שווערעניש. אַלע זענען געוואָרן פֿיַיער־און־פֿלאַם. ס'טייטש, גלייבסט ניש' אַזאַ זאַך. די אַלטסטע גאַנץ פֿראַמפּאָל פֿאַר ליגנער. וואָס האָב איך געזאָלט טון? כ'האָב געגלייבט און זאָל די לצים וווּיל באַקומען.

אַ יתום בין איך געוואָרן. דער זיידע, וואָס האָט מיך געהאָדעוועט, האָט שוין געשמעקט צו דער ערד. בקיצור, מ'האָט מיך אַוועקגעגעבן צו אַ בעקער. נו, פֿרעגט שוין נישׁ' וואָס דאָרט האָט זיך אָפּגעטון. יעדע מויד און יעדעס וויַיבל, וואָס איז געקומען אָפּבאַקן אַ בעקן קיכלעך אָדער

אַ

יך בין גימפל תם. איך האַלט מיך נישט פֿאַר קיין נאַר. פֿאַרקערט. נאָר די לײַט
רופֿן מיך מיט אַזאַ צונעמעניש. מ׳האָט מיך אָנגעהויבן רופֿן אַזוי נאָך אין חדר. זיבן צונעמען האָב
איך געהאַט, װי יתרו: טראָף, חמור־אייזל, האַרפֿלאַקס, לעקיש, גלאָמפּ, שמויגער און תם. דער
לעצטער נאָמען האָט זיך צו מיר צוגעקלעפּט. װאָס איז געװען מײַן נאַרישקייט? באשר מ׳האָט
מיך גרינג געקאָנט אָפּנאַרן. מ׳האָט געזאָגט: גימפּל, דו װייסט, די רביצין איז געלעגן געװאָרן.
בין איך נישט געקומען אין חדר. נו, האָט זיך אַרויסגעװיזן אַז ס׳איז געװען אַ ליגן. פֿון װאַנען
האָב איך דאָס געזאָלט װיסן? װײַל זי האָט נישט געהאַט קיין גראָבן בויך. נו, האָב איך נישט
געקוקט אויף דער רביצינס בויך. איז דאָס אַ נאַרישקייט? אָבער די קונדסים האָבן געלאַכט,
געכיכעט, מיר אַקעגנגעטאַנצט און מיר אָפּגעלייענט אַ קריאת־שמע־לייענען: אל מלך, קאַטשקע

ייִדישע ביכער פֿון יצחק באַשעוויס זינגער

דער שׂטן אין גאָרײַ (1935)

די פֿאַמיליע מושקאַט (1950)

מײַן טאַטנס בית־דין־שטוב (1956)

גימפל תּם און אַנדערע דערצײײלונגען (1963)

דער קנעכט (1967)

דער קונצן־מאַכער פֿון לובלין (1971)

מעשׂיות פֿון הינטערן אויוון (1971)

דער בעל תּשובה (1974)

דער שפּיגל און אַנדערע דערצײײלונגען (1975)

די נאָבעלע רעדע (1979)

שׂונאים, די געשיכטע פֿון אַ ליבע (2022)

דער שאַרלאַטאַן (2022)